Solitary Glen

Redemption Mountain, Book Twenty-Four

Historical Western Romance

SHIRLEEN DAVIES

Books Series by Shirleen Davies

Historical Western Romances
Redemption Mountain
MacLarens of Fire Mountain Historical
MacLarens of Boundary Mountain

Contemporary Western Romance
Cowboys of Whistle Rock Ranch
MacLarens of Fire Mountain
Contemporary
Macklins of Whiskey Bend

Romantic Suspense
Eternal Brethren Military Romantic
Suspense
Peregrine Bay Romantic Suspense

The best way to stay in touch is to subscribe to my newsletter. Visit my Website *www.shirleendavies.com* and fill in your email and name in the Join My Newsletter boxes. That's it!

Description

Duty drives this frontier deputy.
What will happen when duty and desire collide?

Morgan Wheeler lives for his job in Splendor, Montana. He had no idea what would await him upon his arrival two years earlier. Eager to hire more deputies, the sheriff handed him a badge the same day. He's come to love the town and its people. Especially one attractive young woman who spends her days working at the town's orphanage.

Amelia Newhall traveled west, seeking independence from her dominating father. Finding the town more welcoming and generous than anything witnessed back east, she accepted a job at the Eagle's Nest. Three years later, she now works at the town orphanage, finding her job both challenging and fulfilling. Her days are so busy she hardly notices the handsome deputy who volunteers his time.

Or is it her attraction to him she refuses to admit? There is little time to figure it out.

The orphanage is plagued by a series of threats which place the children and adults in imminent danger. Soon after Morgan helps eliminate the risk, another arises. At the same time, the town prepares to battle a merciless gang of roving outlaws.

Putting them in increasing peril is a natural disaster which threatens everything Morgan and Amelia hold dear. Through it all, the two must work together to thwart the threats and keep the children and town safe.

Will their efforts be enough to save those they care about? What will the ongoing struggles mean to the growing feelings between them?

Solitary Glen, book twenty-four in the Redemption Mountain historical western romance series, is a full-length, clean and wholesome novel with an HEA and no cliffhanger.

Table of Contents

Solitary Glen

Chapter One

Morgan crashed through the underbrush, his lungs burning as he pursued the fleeing boy. Leaves and twigs snapped under his boots as he darted between the trees, focused on his quarry.

The boy wove between the trunks ahead of him, glancing back now and then with wide, frightened eyes. Morgan poured on a burst of speed, his longer legs eating up the distance.

As he hurdled a fallen log, Morgan's thoughts drifted briefly back to his siblings, recalling their laughter and mischief when they were young. How his little sisters would beg him to play hide and seek in the barn, stifling giggles as they wedged themselves into bales of hay. His younger brother tagged along, always trying to keep up with his big brother's adventures.

Morgan shook the memories away, narrowing his

1

sights on the orphan boy just ahead. He couldn't let him get away, not when the child had so much to lose by running. The deputy sheriff refused to fail him now.

The boy darted around a cluster of large boulders. Morgan changed direction, veering right, anticipating the move. He collided with the boy, grabbing him firmly by the collar.

"Whoa, there. Settle down." Morgan's gruff voice sounded strained as the boy struggled in his grip. "Where exactly did you think you were running off to?"

The boy just glared up at him, chest heaving from exertion.

"I'm Morgan Wheeler."

"I know who you are. All of us know you're a deputy." He struggled again, Morgan tightening his hold an instant before the boy might've broken loose.

"What's your name?"

"Chad."

Morgan kept a firm hold on the collar as he steered him back toward the orphanage. "Well, Chad, you've got a roof over your head, regular meals, a bed to sleep in. That's more than a lot of kids have. Seems to me running away from some good in your life doesn't make much sense."

Chad looked down, scuffing his feet in the dirt. Morgan felt the boy's resistance fade.

"Let's get you back so Miss Martha can stop worrying herself sick. No one's looking to punish you, son. They just want to keep you safe."

"I'm not your son." Chad blinked back tears as Morgan led him down the path, leaves crunching under their feet once more.

Amelia Newhall stood on the orphanage's back porch, hands on her hips, watching as Morgan emerged from the tree line with the runaway boy in tow. Her face softened when she saw the tears glistening on the boy's cheeks.

"Got our wanderer, I see." Tone light, she hoped to lift the boy's spirits.

Morgan tipped his hat to her as they approached. "Yes, ma'am. He put up quite a chase, but I convinced him his bed here is better than a patch of dirt in the woods."

Amelia smiled at the boy. "Well, you must be hungry after all that running, Chad. Why don't you head inside, and I'll fix you up a plate?"

The boy nodded and hurried past her into the house without a word.

Morgan watched him go, then turned back to Amelia. "That stew I smelled earlier sure had my mouth watering. Would you be willing to spare a bowl for a weary deputy?"

"I believe so," Amelia said with a laugh. "Only if you keep catching our children with itchy feet. Can't have you slacking off in order to fill your belly."

Morgan grinned. "Yes, ma'am. You have my word. Hungry or not, I'll do my best to bring back every last kid who tries to run off."

"Good man. Now, go wash up. While you're gone, I'll ladle up two bowls. One for you and another for

Chad."

Morgan touched the brim of his hat, heart lighter as he watched Amelia disappear into the house. Catching the boy was rewarding. Seeing her smile was his greatest motivation to volunteer at the orphanage.

After filling their stomachs with stew, Morgan escorted the boy to Martha Santori's office. As they entered, she looked up from her desk with a stern expression.

"Chad, what were you thinking by running off? You know we only want what's best for you here. Who knows what would've happened to you if Deputy Wheeler hadn't chased you down."

The boy hung his head, scuffing his shoe on the floor. "I'm sorry, ma'am. I just miss my family."

Morgan's brows rose at the response.

Martha's eyes softened. She stood and put a hand on his shoulder. "I know you do, and I'm sorry they aren't around here anymore. We're your family now. All of us at the orphanage care about you."

"Why not me?" Chad's voice was so soft, she had to lean close to hear.

"What do you mean?"

"Why didn't I die with them when the wagon turned over in the river? Everyone died but me."

She placed a hand on his shoulder. "I don't have an answer for you."

Chad nodded, still looking down.

Martha gently lifted his chin. "No more running, understand? If you're feeling sad or lonely, you come talk to me."

"Yes, ma'am."

"Good. Go outside with the other children. We'll talk more tomorrow."

As he hurried out, Martha turned to Morgan. "Thank you for bringing him back safely. I don't know what we'd do without your help."

He tipped his hat. "Happy to do it, ma'am. Those kids mean a lot to me, too."

After leaving the office, Morgan got to work on his volunteer tasks. He fixed a broken stair rail, chopped firewood, and made minor roof repairs. Working with his hands had always appealed to him.

In between tasks, he took time to interact with the children. He pushed a small girl on the swing set, read a story to a group of young boys and girls, and taught some older kids how to properly whittle wood.

Seeing the smiles on the children's faces while volunteering filled Morgan's heart with joy. This place had become a second home, the children a second family.

He wiped sweat from his brow as he finished repairing the loose shingles on the orphanage's roof. Though it was hard work, he didn't mind lending his skills to maintain the old building. Climbing down the ladder, he noticed Amelia in the yard, hanging laundry on the line to dry.

His pulse quickened at the sight of her. Amelia was different from many young ladies in town—clever, witty, and industrious, with a beauty more than skin deep. Morgan found himself thinking about the pretty cook more and more.

Walking across the yard, he searched for the right words to start a conversation. "Afternoon, Miss Amelia. Sure is a nice day for laundry."

Amelia smiled, her hazel eyes glinting in the sunlight. "It is, indeed, Deputy. Though it's not my favorite task."

Morgan chuckled. "It's not for many of us. The orphanage would probably fall apart if not for your cooking."

Amelia laughed, pinned up another small dress, turning toward Morgan. "Will you be staying for supper tonight? I'm making chicken and dumplings. There will be enough to feed an army or one hungry deputy."

"I'd be honored. Your cooking's the best in the territory." Morgan tipped his hat again, hoping he didn't sound too eager.

While they chatted, Martha Santori watched them from the classroom window, a knowing look on her face. It seemed the deputy's visits to the orphanage were becoming more frequent these days. And she couldn't help but notice how he and Amelia stole glances at each other when they thought no one was looking. Young love, Martha mused, before turning to her office.

By late afternoon, the children were out for play-time before supper. Morgan set aside his tools and joined them in the yard, initiating a rowdy game of tag. His booming laughter mingled with the children's delighted squeals as they chased each other around the grounds.

When tiny Betsy tripped and skinned her knee, Morgan scooped her up and soothed away her tears. "There now, it's just a scratch." He cleaned up the wound before setting her down. She beamed up at him, her tears forgotten.

As twilight fell, Martha rang the bell, calling everyone in for supper. He herded the children inside, sneaking playful tickles along the way. His gaze met Amelia's through the kitchen window. They exchanged smiles.

Morgan lingered on the back porch as the last of the children filed inside for supper. The fading light cast shadows across the yard as a light breeze rustled the shimmering leaves of the graceful aspen trees.

He breathed in the crisp evening air, feeling a tired contentment. This place had become dear to him in the months since he began volunteering. He never would have imagined it when he first rode into Splendor two years earlier with his best friends, Jonas and Tucker.

Lost in thought, he didn't notice Amelia until she stepped beside him. "It's a nice evening, isn't it?"

Morgan turned to her with a smile. "Sure is. The end of a good day."

They stood in easy silence for a moment, watching

the shadows lengthen across the yard. Amelia tucked a strand of hair behind her ear. "Supper's ready."

"I'll be right in."

She met his eyes, her expression soft. "I better get back to the kitchen. See you inside."

Morgan watched her go, his heart skipping a beat. When she closed the door, he released a slow breath, looking up at the first stars against the darkening sky.

With a last look around the peaceful yard, he headed inside, the sounds of laughter and happy chatter welcoming him.

So similar to family suppers back home, he thought, before heading toward an empty chair.

Finding a seat among the children, he knew this was where he belonged. For the first time in a long while, he looked forward to what tomorrow might bring.

Chapter Two

Morgan rose early the next morning, the predawn light starting to creep over the mountains. After a quick breakfast, he headed out to make his rounds. Splendor was quiet this early, the streets empty except for a few shopkeepers opening their doors.

After stopping at the jail, he walked along Frontier Street, slowing to look behind him. Four covered wagons made their way down the street, anxious faces peering out of the front and back. He wondered where they were headed and where they'd been.

Watching until they stopped near the livery, he crossed the street toward Suzanne's boardinghouse. He spotted his best friends and fellow deputies, Jonas Taylor and Tucker Nolan, at a table inside. They motioned for him to join them.

Ordering coffee, he glanced around at the other patrons chatting over their morning meals before turning his attention back to his friends seated across from him.

"So, anything interesting happen in town yesterday while I was at the orphanage?"

Jonas shook his head as he swallowed a mouthful of biscuit. "Nah, pretty quiet day. I did hear talk of more folks arriving on the afternoon stagecoach. Seems like every day brings more settlers looking to stake a claim out here."

"It's the fever of westward expansion," Tucker said, using his fork to gesture as he spoke. "Back east, newspapers and pamphlets make Montana out to be the land of milk and honey. Folks are eager to make a new start."

Morgan nodded thoughtfully. More newcomers meant more potential for trouble. And more competition for land and jobs. He made a mental note to speak to Horace at the bank to get his take on the situation.

"Well, I best finish my rounds." Morgan pushed back his chair and stood. "I'll see you boys later."

Stepping out onto Frontier Street's now bustling boardwalk, the morning sun glinted off the windows of the shops and buildings lining the rutted road. He nodded in greeting at the familiar faces, receiving smiles in return.

His first stop was the general store owned by Stan Petermann. A bell chimed overhead as he pushed through the door into the well-stocked store. Stan looked up from behind the counter and broke into a grin.

"Morgan, good to see you." He came around to pump Morgan's hand. "What can I do for you today?"

Though he saw the shopkeeper nearly every day

on his rounds, the man's friendliness never wavered. Stan had been in Splendor for years, knew most of the people, and was part of the town leadership group. The man kept tabs on the comings and goings, and had an opinion on just about everything.

"Just stopping in to check on things. Anything new around town?"

Stan's expression grew more serious as he leaned on the counter. "Well, now, I've been wondering about all these folks moving out west lately. Seems every day more wagons roll into town. New faces everywhere you look."

Morgan nodded, recalling the caravan he'd seen earlier.

"It's the same all over. This recession back east has people fleeing for better opportunities," Stan continued. "This kind of growth can't come without growing pains for a place like Splendor. We're a tight community here. I hope these newcomers don't disrupt what we've built."

Morgan understood his wariness. Their frontier town had preserved its close-knit feel even as it expanded.

"It's real hard not to change when a town grows," Morgan said. "Look at any of the towns back east. They were once small. Look at them now. They've gotten so big, they're pushing people out."

"Too right, Deputy." Stan glanced out the window of his shop. "Too darned right."

After chatting a few minutes more, Morgan continued his rounds, thoughts swirling about Stan's concerns over the influx of settlers.

He tipped his hat to passersby, exchanging friendly greetings. At the telegraph office, he stepped inside the small clapboard building.

"Good morning, Bernie," Morgan said to the long-time telegraph operator and post office clerk.

Bouncing on the balls of his feet, Bernie grinned. "Deputy Wheeler, good to see you. Here to send one of your money orders back east?"

Morgan nodded, pulling some bills from his pocket. "Need to do what I can."

Bernie counted the money and filled out a money order form, showing it to Morgan. "I'll get this off on today's stage."

"Appreciate it."

Tucking the receipt into his shirt pocket, he returned to the boardwalk. Their mother had died birthing the youngest sister. Ever since their father had passed, his siblings depended on the money he sent. He wished it was more, but the letters from home assured Morgan anything he sent was welcome.

He surveyed the busy street. A rumbling sound approached from behind him. Two more covered wagons rolled into view, canvas billowing and wooden wheels creaking over the hard-packed dirt.

Eager faces looked out, newcomers with hopeful eyes. Children waved enthusiastically at townsfolk they passed. Morgan watched, taking in the meager belongings lashed to the wagons. As thousands of others, these settlers had left everything behind for a new start out west.

He understood the yearning for a better life. For the second time in a few hours, he wondered where the people were headed.

Stan's warning about growing pains stuck in his head.

Morgan continued on his rounds, thoughts swirling about the newcomers to Splendor. Was it truly as dire as Stan made it sound?

He stopped in front of the bank, hoping to speak with Horace Clausen. As president, Horace was often the first to know about changes in Splendor, and loved sharing his predictions. He would have insight into what was driving these settlers west.

Pushing through the carved wooden door, he stepped into the hushed interior. Horace sat scribbling at his desk. He glanced up, face breaking into a smile beneath his graying mustache.

"Morgan, good to see you. What brings you by today?"

He settled into the leather chair across from Horace. "I wanted your take about all the wagons rolling into town. It seems more folks are lighting out west lately. Why's that?"

Horace's easy smile slid away as he folded his hands on his desk. "It's this blasted recession back east. Started last year. Banks foreclosing, jobs disappearing. For many, heading west is the only hope left." He sighed. "Word's spread about places like Splendor offering a fresh start. Due to my friends and colleagues back east, I've had inquiries from dozens of families eager to settle here." Leaning forward, Horace met Morgan's gaze. "Big changes are coming. I hope Splendor's ready. This growth may challenge us in ways we haven't considered."

Morgan absorbed this, brow furrowed. He loved Splendor. He also understood the hopelessness driving people west.

"How many do you figure actually stay in this area?"

"As opposed to continuing on to Idaho, Utah, or California?"

Morgan nodded.

"It's hard to say. I've handled about three sales this month alone. Most of the time, one sale a month is average. Plus, I'm working with Noah, Gabe, and a few others to expand the number of stores and such. Though many will pass through, we'll get our share of newcomers."

"We'll make it work."

Horace smiled. "You're a good man with the best intentions and the right attitude. Gabe has assembled a fine group of people. I'm certain you and the other deputies will be enough to get us through the surge of settlers." Glancing at the man in a black suit and black ribbon tie approaching his desk, he shook Morgan's hand. "My appointment is here. Glad you came by, Deputy."

Morgan stepped outside, lowering his hat against the late morning sun. His boots echoed on the boardwalk as he made his way down Frontier Street, lost in thought.

Horace's words rolled around in his head. Change

was coming. That much was clear. Wagon trains packed with hopeful settlers were arriving almost weekly.

How many would stay was a mystery, though it was certain Splendor's quality would appeal to some. Soon, the town's quiet streets would be bustling with newcomers.

Nearing the sheriff's office, his gaze lingered on familiar storefronts. As much as he wanted to protect and preserve Splendor's special character, he feared it might be impossible.

The recession back east had left people with few choices. How could he resent them for seeking better lives out west?

He stepped into the sheriff's office, the smell of coffee greeting him. Jonas looked up from a stack of wanted posters.

"Coffee's hot if you want some."

Morgan nodded and filled a steaming cup, taking a grateful sip.

"Town's been peaceful so far today." Jonas leaned back in the chair. "Though with all these new folks arriving, who knows how long that'll last."

"My thoughts exactly. I already had an earful from Horace at the bank."

Jonas chuckled. "Let me guess. The man sees doom around every corner."

"Maybe so. He seemed resigned to the growth." He looked out the window as another wagon rolled past the jail. "Change is coming, no doubt about it. We best be ready."

Jonas's expression grew serious. "Ready for what, exactly? Do you really think newcomers are going to cause trouble?"

Morgan considered the question. Most settlers wanted a decent living and a place to call home. "Not intentionally. But any time a small town grows fast, it can strain things. We may see more crime. Theft, public drunkenness. Maybe worse."

Jonas looked thoughtful. "You could be right."

"I wonder what Gabe thinks?"

Jonas nodded. "With his contacts back east, the sheriff often knows more about what's coming than anyone else."

"Him and Horace Clausen." Morgan stepped to the window, watching the now crowded street in a different way.

Chapter Three

Amelia stepped out of the general store, juggling three packages. Adjusting them in her arms, she nearly collided with Morgan Wheeler on the boardwalk.

"Whoa, there." Morgan tipped his hat. "Good morning, Miss Amelia."

"Good morning, Deputy," Amelia replied with a smile. "So sorry. I should pay better attention to where I'm going."

They fell into step together, strolling down the busy boardwalk.

"I hear there are two more boys coming in from the Big Pine orphanage," Morgan said. "That'll make close to twenty at the Splendor orphanage."

"Yes, we're making room as best we can. I just hope we can provide all the care and comfort those poor children need."

Their conversation was interrupted by angry shouts from across the street. Outside the land office, two men were nose-to-nose, gesturing wildly as their argument escalated.

Morgan's jaw tightened, his easy smile replaced by a look of concern. People were stopping to stare, crowding around the enraged men.

"This doesn't look good," Morgan muttered. He touched the brim of his hat. "Excuse me, Miss Amelia."

Morgan recognized the two men as Teddy Minor and Jeb Stokes, two hardheaded ranchers who'd been feuding over land and water for years.

Amelia watched Morgan rush across the street, narrowly avoiding a passing wagon. On the board-walk, Teddy pulled his right arm back, the recoiled fist landed with an audible thud on Jeb's chin. Teetering, Jeb found his footing, lowering his head to plow into Teddy when Morgan charged between them.

"No fighting in town." His hands rose in a calming gesture.

Teddy jabbed a finger at Jeb. "This thief's stealin' water that isn't his!"

"You're a darned liar!" Jeb spat back. "That creek runs through my land fair and square."

Morgan kept his voice steady. "I know you boys have had your disagreements in the past. But we've got a whole town of onlookers here. No good's gonna come from letting this get out of hand."

He put a hand on each man's shoulder. "Now, I'm not taking sides. I aim to keep the peace. Let's talk this out inside the land office, or I'll have to insist you both get moving."

The men shrugged off Morgan's touch, but his words had hit their mark. The fight went out of them as they realized how public their spat had become.

With a disgruntled snort, Teddy stomped off toward the saloon. Jeb lingered a moment, glaring after his rival.

"We aren't done with this," Jeb muttered before heading off in the opposite direction.

Morgan watched the two ranchers disappear down opposite ends of the street, the tension lingering in the air. He knew this dispute was a tinderbox ready to explode if he didn't find a way to resolve it.

As Morgan pondered his next move, Deputy Tucker Nolan rode up and dismounted next to him. "Heard there was some trouble over here. Everything all right?"

Morgan filled Tucker in on the disagreement between the two ranchers. "It's the water rights issue again. Only going to get worse if someone doesn't settle it."

Tucker nodded, peering down the street. "Hotheads like them two won't back down easy. We best keep an eye out, make sure their disagreement doesn't turn into something uglier."

"I know Teddy's got a surplus from the creek on his land. Jeb's herd doubled in size this season," Morgan said. "He's desperate to get more water."

"And Teddy aims to hold onto every drop he's got." Tucker shook his head. "Sheriff's gonna have a heck of a time working this out. And we'll be the ones confronting good men who stand on the wrong side of a decision." Tucker flashed a rueful grin. "Just another day keeping the peace in Splendor, huh?"

Morgan chuckled as they headed back across the street. "Wouldn't have it any other way, partner."

Reaching the boardwalk on the other side, Morgan stopped. "I'm going to talk to Miss Amelia. Are you fine talking to Gabe about what happened?"

Tucker glanced behind him at the woman standing outside the general store. "My pleasure."

Morgan's boots thudded on the wooden boardwalk as he strode toward her. His jaw was set, brow furrowed. The argument between the ranchers had put him in a sour mood.

"Everything all right?" Concern creased Amelia's face.

He sighed, running a hand through his hair. "Yeah. A spat over water rights. We encouraged them to work something out when the whole town wasn't listening." He met her gaze.

Her warm brown eyes and gentle smile made some of the tension ease from his shoulders.

"According to the sheriff, those two have been feuding over water and property lines for years. I'm not certain there's a good solution for anyone. It could become a bigger issue with all the newcomers arriving."

Amelia gave a slow nod. "I can understand why they'd be on edge. Still, fisticuffs don't seem the Christian way to settle disagreements."

Morgan barked out a laugh. "No, ma'am. But Teddy Minor and Jeb Stokes aren't known for their manners."

Their conversation was interrupted by a sudden shout. Morgan's head snapped around to see Teddy Minor barreling toward Jeb Stokes, fist cocked back. Before Morgan could react, Teddy let fly and landed a solid punch to Jeb's jaw.

The small crowd who hadn't dispersed gasped as Jeb reeled from the blow. Righting himself, Jeb stormed toward Teddy, head down as he rammed into his neighbor's chest. Both men went down, rolling off the boardwalk and onto the street.

In a flash, Morgan hauled a struggling Teddy away from his rival. Tucker rushed to intervene before Jeb could retaliate.

"That's enough!" Morgan muscled his way between the two men. "I said your business here is done! Do we have to haul you to the jail?"

Jeb spat blood into the street, his eyes blazing. "This ain't over, Minor! You'll get yours soon enough."

Teddy strained against Morgan's hold, teeth bared. "Anytime, Stokes! I'll be waitin'."

Morgan put a hand firmly on Jeb's chest, holding him back. "Mount up and get, the both of you!" He glared at each man in turn. "Take this feud elsewhere, before you end up spending the night in jail."

With Tucker's help, Morgan kept the ranchers separated. Still trading threats and insults, Jeb and Teddy swung onto their horses, riding toward opposite ends of the main street.

Morgan watched them disappear in clouds of

dust, a muscle flickering along his jawline. He'd hoped the day's violence was over, even as a bad feeling formed in his gut.

Letting out a weary sigh, he turned to Tucker, who was brushing dirt from his sleeves with a disgruntled look.

"Hard to believe those two came from the same family," Tucker remarked.

"Second cousins?"

"I believe so. The Stokes and Minors have never gotten along. I'm not sure, but I've heard the initial feud began over property lines and water rights. Guess nothing's changed."

Morgan nodded grimly. "I'm afraid it's going to get worse."

"Agreed." Tucker kicked a loose pebble down the road. "I'd better get to the jail before Gabe leaves."

Morgan cast a look toward the spot where Amelia had been waiting. Disappointment tugged when he saw she was gone. Sighing, he crossed his arms, lips pressed in a thin line as one more wagon rolled through town.

Tucker watched, reading his friend's thoughts. They'd do their duty, even if it meant standing between bad-tempered ranchers. The lawmen shared one last resolute look before heading their separate ways, spirits steeled for the struggle ahead.

Amelia met Martha at their wagon a few minutes later for the ride back to the orphanage. She'd watched the fight and aftermath as long as she could before hurrying to the livery.

Fights weren't uncommon in Splendor, though she never got used to seeing grown men go after each other with such violence. At least no one had pulled a gun.

"Are you ready?" Martha watched her set the parcels in the back along with some tools Noah Brandt suggested for repairs.

"I am." Climbing onto the seat next to Martha, Amelia thought of the fight. "Have you seen many fights in town?"

"A few. Why?" Martha slapped the lines, driving the wagon south out of town.

"Morgan had to break up a fight outside the land office. Two ranchers were shouting. The men walked away from each other as if they were done. Morgan walked over to talk to me, and the men started up again. This time, they ended up rolling around on the street, punching and kicking each other."

"And Morgan had to break them up again?"

"Morgan and Tucker Nolan."

Martha slapped the lines a little harder to get the horses moving. "I know Tucker."

"Well, they pulled the men apart. I couldn't hear what was said, but the two men got on their horses and rode off. And you should've seen the people crowded around them. It was as if they were watching children play."

"Most men settle disputes by talking. Others by fighting. It's the way things are, Amelia."

"I wonder if Morgan's ever been in a fight."

"He's a deputy, and I know he has a couple brothers back home in Ohio. Logic would say he has been in a fight or two."

The wagon jolted over the rutted road for several minutes before Amelia broke the silence.

"What do you think of Morgan?"

Martha hid a grin. "In what way?"

"I don't know." She concentrated on the road ahead, her brows drawing together. "Well, as a person, I suppose."

Martha pretended to think a moment, knowing what Amelia was asking. "First of all, I like Morgan. He's honest, is a hard worker, and loves being around the children. There's nothing to dislike about him. Why are you asking?"

"No real reason. I'm curious about him is all." Amelia's lips drew into a thin line as she pictured him rushing between the two men, breaking up the fight. "Just curious."

Chapter Four

Dorinda and her six-year-old son, Joel, walked with haste through town, their footsteps echoing in the quiet morning air. As the lone teacher, her classroom included children of all ages. A fact which encouraged her early arrival to organize the various lessons.

"Uncle Spencer said I might be able to help birth a calf next week." Joel could barely contain his excitement. "He said I could name it, too."

Dorinda smiled at the boy's enthusiasm, not mentioning they'd have to be at Redemption's Edge ranch for Joel to watch. "Sounds like quite the adventure."

"I miss living on the ranch." Joel's wistful tone hit Dorinda in the chest. "I loved riding my horse whenever I wanted." He kicked a small rock he spotted on the boardwalk onto the road. "When can we move back?"

She knew the ranch held a special place in Joel's heart. It reminded him of their farm back in Utah. The home they'd left when her dutiful Mormon husband took a second wife. The hurt of his broken promise still plagued her.

"I know this move hasn't been easy for you. Perhaps in time, you might grow to appreciate certain parts of town. More children your age to play with, for one. And I promise, we'll visit your uncle as often as we can."

Joel sighed. "Yeah, I guess."

As if she'd summoned them up, a group of boys ran past, laughing and shouting. She gave Joel's shoulder a reassuring squeeze.

"See? Town life has some advantages. Now, let's get you to school so I can get prepared, and you can tell your friends all about the calf you'll be birthing next week."

His face brightened a bit. The two picked up their pace, continuing toward the schoolhouse.

As they rounded a corner, Joel spotted the group of boys playing in the street, dashing to the side when riders approached. He glanced up at his mother.

"How come we can't live at the ranch all the time again?" he asked.

She paused, forcing patience over a conversation repeated many times. "Well, the ranch is too far to travel every day. And because of bad weather, there are days I wouldn't be able to get to the schoolhouse at all. Remember, Joel, I'm the teacher, and the other children depend on me."

He scowled. "School's boring. I learn more doing stuff on the ranch."

"Yes, ranch life teaches many valuable skills. Book learning is equally important. When you're older, you'll be glad you have both."

He didn't look convinced. Dorinda ruffled his hair affectionately.

"Give it time. You might find you enjoy school more than you think."

They paused when she noticed an elderly man sitting on a bench outside the jail. He was dressed in an ill-fitting, dusty black suit that had seen better days. His wrinkled face was weathered, his hands shaking enough to notice.

Curious, she altered her path and approached the man. "Good morning."

The old man looked up, his pale eyes crinkling at the corners as he tipped his hat. "Good morning to you, as well."

Her eyes widened at his formal speech. "I don't believe we've met. I'm Dorinda Heaton, and this is my son, Joel."

"Enoch Weaver."

"Pleased to make your acquaintance, Mr. Weaver."

"Likewise." Enoch shifted on the bench to face her more fully. "It seems I've seen you and the boy talking with the deputies. You're somewhat new in town, correct?"

"Yes, we moved here last Christmas from Utah. My brother, Spencer, works for the Pelletiers, so we lived there until I accepted the teaching position. Joel is still getting used to town life. He misses the ranch."

Enoch nodded knowingly. "I can't say I blame the lad. The town's all right. However, there are many advantages to ranch life. The animals and quiet solitude makes life on a ranch something special."

"It sounds like you have experience with ranch living," she said.

"Not really. I was an attorney back home before..." His voice trailed off for a moment.

"Before moving to Splendor. I had friends who owned ranches and farms. There were many times I envied their lives."

She looked down at her son. "We were talking about the ranch this morning. He was going on about all the animals and the freedom, right, Joel?"

"Yes, ma'am."

Enoch chuckled. "You can't cage a wild spirit for long. The ranch may always call to him." He grew thoughtful. "Town living has merits, too, even for a young man like you, Joel. More and more children are moving into town. You'll make many friends here."

"Yes, sir." Joel sighed.

Dorinda nodded her agreement. She found herself taking an instant liking to this man who so clearly understood both her and Joel's perspectives.

Deputy Dutch McFarlin emerged from the jailhouse, his boots sounding on the wooden steps. He tipped his hat to them as he approached.

"Morning, folks. Heading to school, I see." He smiled at Dorinda and Joel.

"That's right, Deputy," she replied. "And how are you today?"

"I'm doing well, so far. I'll be busy later with the

usual petty squabbles and mischief around town. I swear, some days it feels like I'm dealing with a bunch of children." He laughed good-naturedly. "No offense, ma'am."

She chuckled. "None taken. I can only imagine how difficult your job can be. Children of any age will be children, I'm afraid."

Dutch nodded. "How are you settling in as the new teacher? I know it can't be easy coming into an unfamiliar town and taking charge of a classroom."

"It's a challenge," Dorinda admitted. "But the children are eager to learn, and the town has been so welcoming. I'm starting to feel at home."

"That's real good to hear," Dutch said, sincerity clear in his deep voice.

When the church bells chimed the hour, Dorinda regretfully took her leave, thanking Enoch for the enlightening conversation. Dutch fell into step beside them as she and Joel ambled toward the schoolhouse.

"You know, when I first arrived a few years back, this town was little more than a few ramshackle buildings and a saloon. But we've come a long way since then."

Dutch told a story about one particular situation about local miners and a party they'd planned in town. Joel listened with rapt attention, his eyes shining as Dutch described apprehending belligerent drunk miners and chasing rowdy cowboys out of town.

Dorinda found herself warming to the deputy's affable manner. As they approached the small, whitewashed schoolhouse, Dutch's pace slowed. His sharp eyes narrowed, focusing on a cluster of bushes near the entrance. He thought he saw movement. A flash of color that didn't belong.

Resting his hand on his holstered pistol, he turned off the path toward the shrubbery. As he drew nearer, two small faces peered out at him.

"Well, now. What do we have here?" Dutch said, his voice friendly, though firm.

The children, a boy and girl who looked to be around Joel's age, glanced at each other. Before he could say another word, they bolted from their hiding spot and took off running.

"Hey, now, hold on!" he called after them, before glancing back at Dorinda and Joel. "I'll be back as soon as I can. Got a couple of strays to round up."

He tipped his hat and set off after the fleeing children, his long strides closing the distance. They led him on a merry chase, but Dutch's keen eye and persistence won out.

Breathing hard, the boy and girl finally stopped, realizing they couldn't outrun the tenacious lawman. Dutch approached, hands raised in a calming gesture.

"Easy now, I won't hurt you. I'd sure like to know what you're doing out here all by your lonesome. Where are your folks?"

The children glanced at each other again, a silent conversation passing between them. After a moment, the girl stepped forward, her expression resolute. "We ain't got no folks, mister. It's just me and my brother now."

Dutch's eyes softened with understanding. He crouched down so he was at eye level with the children. "Well, now, that's a mighty sad thing to hear. What're your names?"

The girl jutted her chin out in defiance. "I'm Wilma. This here's my brother, Harry."

Harry peeked out from behind his sister, regarding the lawman with caution.

"Pleased to meet you both," Dutch said. "I'm Deputy Dutch McFarlin. Now, I know you're scared, but running away won't solve anything. Why don't you come with me, and we'll see about finding you a warm meal?"

Wilma looked uncertain, gripping her brother's hand. Dutch was patient, sensing their indecision.

Harry looked at his sister, pleading in a small voice. "We're so hungry, Wilma."

Her shoulders slumped in resignation. She met Dutch's earnest gaze and nodded. "All right, mister. We'll go with you."

Dutch smiled and stood. "You've made the right choice."

As they walked, he kept up a steady stream of lighthearted chatter to help put them at ease. He pointed out landmarks and familiar faces, weaving humorous anecdotes about the town's residents. Wilma and Harry's shy smiles emerged as he spoke.

As they neared the sheriff's office, Dutch sensed the children tense up again. "No need to worry now. Sheriff Evans may look intimidating, but he has a heart of gold when it comes to children."

Gabe looked up as Dutch entered with the children. His expression softened when he took in their bedraggled appearance.

"Well, now, who do we have here?"

Dutch made quick introductions. "This is Wilma and her brother, Harry. I found them hiding outside the schoolhouse this morning. They're alone and in need of some care."

Gabe's keen eyes studied the orphans. "Hmm, is that so?" He stood up and came around his desk, crouching down. "You've had a rough time. Deputy McFarlin will find you a hot meal and a place to sleep for tonight. We'll sort the rest out tomorrow."

Wilma blinked back tears. She stiffened her spine and nodded.

Gabe smiled as he straightened. "Suzanne will feed them, then you'll need to get them out to Martha Santori. She'll know what to do."

Dutch tipped his hat. "Will do."

He escorted Wilma and Harry to the boardinghouse run by Suzanne Barnett. She ran a restaurant attached to the boardinghouse, where he took many of his meals.

Suzanne listened as he described their situation. "It just so happens I have plenty of eggs, bacon, and potatoes." She looked down at the children. "How does that sound?"

They nodded eagerly. "We ain't had a proper meal in days," Wilma said.

"Well, don't worry. There's plenty to eat here." She turned to Dutch, lowering her voice. "I suppose you'll try to find out who they belong to?"

"Yes, ma'am. I'll track down any information I can." He looked at Wilma and Harry. "When they're finished eating, I'll take them out to Martha. Do you mind watching them for a few minutes?"

Suzanne touched his arm. "We'll take fine care of them until you get back."

"Where you going, mister?" The uncertainty in Wilma's voice sliced through him.

"I'll be back real soon, and we'll head out to a place with lots of beds and good people to watch over you. You two be good for Mrs. Barnett. Understand?"

The children nodded, their small faces pinched with worry.

"I promise I'll be back." This seemed to calm them.

He watched Suzanne usher them into the kitchen before leaving to learn what he could about them.

As he made his way toward the telegraph office, someone calling his name made him turn. Dorinda rushed toward him, her face lined with concern.

"What did you find, Deputy McFarlin?"

Dutch explained about the brother and sister he'd found hiding in the bushes. He chose not to include the chase into town.

"Those poor children, having to fend for themselves." Her voice was gentle but firm. "What can I do to help?"

Dutch smiled. "I was just headed to send some wires about our new friends. It'd be a big help if you could ask the children if they've seen Wilma and

Harry before."

"I'll be happy to, and will let you know if I learn anything."

"Thank you, Mrs. Heaton. I'm going to send a telegram to the orphanage in Big Pine, though it's hard to imagine those children getting this far without anyone noticing. If you'll excuse me..."

"Of course. I'll be in touch."

Dutch walked to the telegraph office. Bernie looked up from his paperwork, continuing to tap his pencil on the counter as his gaze darted around the small room.

"Afternoon, Dutch. What can I do for you?"

Stepping forward, he removed his hat. "I need to send a telegram to the orphanage in Big Pine about a couple of kids we found. No one seems to know who they are or where they came from. Maybe the people there will have some information."

Bernie's eyebrows shot up before he scribbled the message on a pad. Dutch provided details on the children's approximate ages and appearances. Finishing, Bernie rocked back on his heels as he read.

"That cover it?"

Dutch nodded. "Fine."

He walked outside, knowing all he could do was wait and hope someone responded. The truth was another orphan appeared every few weeks, stretching the capacity of the Splendor orphanage. The odds Wilma and Harry would be added to those already there thudded in his chest.

Chapter Five

Dutch arrived at the orphanage at noon. Seated beside him were Wilma and Harry, anxiously holding each other's hand. He'd learned their ages from Suzanne. Wilma had turned six a few weeks earlier, while Harry would be five after Thanksgiving. Younger than Dutch had originally thought.

As they approached the front porch, the door swung open. Martha emerged, flanked by Amelia, both with broad smiles. Dutch tipped his hat in greeting.

"Afternoon, ladies."

"It's good to see you, Deputy McFarlin. Who do you have with you?" Martha kept her gaze on the children as she navigated the steps to the ground.

"A couple young'uns who need a place to stay."

"Happy to have them." She smiled at the children, walking to their side of the wagon. "I'm Mrs. Santori. And this is Miss Amelia."

Dutch jumped to the ground, holding out his arms for Harry.

When the boy hesitated, Wilma nudged him. "It's all right. Go on, now."

He allowed Dutch to carry him up the steps before setting him down. "This is Harry, and the little miss is Wilma, his older sister. They lost their folks a while back."

Martha's gaze returned to Wilma. "May I help you down?"

Saying nothing for a few seconds, Wilma scooted to the edge of the seat, allowing Martha to help her to the ground. Running up the steps, she took her brother's hand, before looking at Dutch.

"It's going to be all right, Wilma. Mrs. Santori will take good care of you."

Martha placed her hands lightly on the children's backs and guided them inside. Dutch hesitated, then followed them into the foyer.

"Ma'am, there are a few things you should know," he said in a low voice.

Martha held up her hand. "Amelia, please introduce Wilma and Harry to the other children, then show them where they'll sleep."

"Of course." Amelia smiled at the two. "Please come with me, and I'll get you settled in."

When they were out of earshot, Martha looked at Dutch. "Sorry. I didn't know what you were going to say."

"No problem. You were protecting the children. There's no easy way to say this, except their daddy was caught up with some dangerous men. The same men who gunned him and his wife down in Big Pine.

I don't know if anyone will come looking, but you should keep an eye out."

"How did you find this out?"

"I sent a telegram to the couple who run the orphanage in Big Pine. They got right back to me. Wilma and Harry were placed with them. An older couple offered to adopt Harry but wasn't interested in Wilma. So..."

"They ran away," Martha finished for him. "How do two young children make it from Big Pine to Splendor by themselves?"

Dutch chuckled. "Gabe asked Big Pine's sheriff, Parker Sterling, to ask the stage clerk if he knew about two children. Seems an older couple took pity on the two and bought them tickets. Apparently, Wilma told them their parents were in Splendor. The children disappeared within minutes of reaching town. They've been living on the streets for about three days."

Martha nodded, her expression serious. "She's a clever girl. I've learned never to underestimate the determination of young children. They surprise me all the time." She nodded at Amelia when she emerged from the kitchen to show the children upstairs.

"We'll be cautious. And I'll make certain Amelia and Rose know about the men. Thank you for bringing them to us, Deputy."

"I know you'll do a fine job making a home for them." When he turned to leave, a cry came from the stairs an instant before someone slammed into his legs.

Dutch glanced down at Harry to see the boy's arms wrapped around him. He stared up at him, his wide eyes glistening with unshed tears. Dutch ruffled the boy's hair as Wilma joined them.

"You listen to Mrs. Santori now. I'll come visit real soon."

Harry tightened his hold around Dutch's legs in a fierce hug. He gently pried him off. "Go on, now. Be good."

When he closed the door behind him, Amelia approached Wilma and Harry.

"Let's get you settled," she said gently. "Now that you've met the other children, I'll show you around the rest of your new home."

She led them through the cozy rooms, pointing out the dining hall, classroom, and library. Wilma clung nervously to Harry's hand while the boy stared around with wide eyes.

Amelia brought them outside to a spacious fenced yard, where a group of children laughed and played games. "You'll have a lot of time to play. We have chores, too, but mostly, it's fun."

Wilma finally gave a timid smile. Back inside, Amelia showed them two empty beds side by side.

"We have two bedrooms for boys and two for girls. For now, you two will sleep next to each other in here. It's one of the girls' rooms. I know it's different, but you'll be safe here." When she turned to look at the children, Harry had disappeared.

Dutch made it halfway down the porch steps before he heard the sound of running footsteps behind him. He turned to see Harry bounding after him, a stricken look on the boy's face.

"Don't go, Mr. Dutch!" Harry cried, flinging his arms around the deputy's legs for a second time. "Please stay with us!"

Dutch's heart twisted at the child's distress. He gently pried Harry's hands off his legs and knelt down. "Harry, we talked about this. I can't stay, but Miss Amelia and Mrs. Santori are going to take real good care of you."

Fat tears rolled down Harry's cheeks. "But I want you!"

With a sigh, Dutch put a hand on the boy's shoulder. "I know it's scary being in a new place. But you're one of the bravest little boys I've ever known. You'll make new friends and have all kinds of adventures."

Harry hiccupped.

"And I'll come visit when I can," Dutch promised. "To see how you're getting on. My job is out there, son, keeping the good folks of Splendor safe."

At last, Harry nodded, wiping his eyes with a grubby fist. Dutch stood, setting a hand on the boy's shoulder.

"You'll do just fine, son. Your ma and pa would be so proud of you."

With that, he tipped his hat at Amelia, who'd watched the exchange from the doorway, and walked down the steps toward his waiting horse.

As Dutch rode back into town, the orphanage grew smaller behind him. He felt the familiar weight of duty settle on his shoulders, knowing he had responsibilities in Splendor he couldn't shirk.

Up ahead, Morgan was lost in thought as he rode toward the orphanage, reflecting on the impact his volunteer work had on him. Though he sent money home to his siblings when he could, visiting those orphaned children stirred an almost paternal protectiveness in him. Their laughter and unconditional affection filled a void he hadn't realized was there.

As he guided his horse farther away from town, Morgan spotted Dutch coming toward him. He nodded in greeting as he pulled up alongside the other man.

"Afternoon, Dutch. Did you visit the orphanage?"

Dutch nodded. "Dropped two new orphans off. They seem like good kids. I'm sure they'll settle in fine with Martha, Amelia, and Rose looking after them."

Morgan made a sound of agreement. "They have a way with children, that's for sure. I'm heading out there to make some repairs. I usually end up staying through supper, reading stories to those interested."

"It's good work you're doing," Dutch said. "I've been thinking I should lend a hand, too, when duty permits."

"I'm sure Martha would appreciate any help you can give them. There are always repairs to be made. And the children crave attention." He paused, growing serious. "It's rewarding work, Dutch. Fulfilling, in a different way than our jobs."

Dutch tugged at his hat brim, looking thoughtful. "Understood. I'll stop by the next chance I get and talk with Martha. I'd best get going."

The two men continued on in separate directions. Morgan arrived at the orphanage, eager to make some headway on the long list of repairs. He found a broken desk in one of the classrooms and set to work mending a drawer and one rickety leg.

As he tinkered, a few curious children gathered around to watch. Morgan smiled at them and asked about their day, listening with interest as they chattered about their lessons and games. When he finished with the desk, he closed the toolbox Noah Brandt had provided for the orphanage.

"Who wants a story?" he asked. A chorus of "Me!" rose up as the children scrambled onto benches. Morgan grinned and launched into a dramatic retelling of Jack and the Beanstalk, much to their delight.

Afterward, he joined Amelia on the front porch. She smiled at his appearance. "Thank you again for your help, Morgan. I don't know what we'd do without you."

He waved off her praise. "Happy to do it. Just wish I could be around more often."

"We all know you have a regular job. Any time you

can spare here is welcome."

They chatted for a bit, enjoying the late afternoon sun. After a spell, the conversation lulled into a comfortable silence.

Amelia's expression turned serious. "There is one thing I wanted to mention. We've had a group of rough-looking men riding by the past few days. They haven't caused any trouble, but..." She trailed off, looking uneasy.

His brows drew together. "Have they done or said anything to you or anyone else?"

"Not that I know of. I haven't said anything to Martha or Rose. Perhaps I should."

"You definitely should. I'll keep an eye out and let Gabe and the other deputies know. You let me know if they give you any grief."

She nodded gratefully. "I'm sure it's nothing to worry about."

"I understand." He hesitated. "You know you can always send for me if you need help."

Amelia smiled. "I appreciate that. Hopefully, it won't come to that. I should get back to the kitchen. Will you stay for supper?"

"Can't tonight. Next time?"

"Anytime..." she answered as the door closed behind her.

Morgan watched her leave before walking to his horse and mounting up. Straightening, he spotted four men riding up the road toward the orphanage. He studied them closely as they approached, wondering if they were the same group Amelia mentioned.

From a deputy's perspective, the men looked like trouble. Morgan nudged his horse forward to intercept them before they reached the front porch.

"Afternoon, gentlemen," Morgan called out, keeping his voice steady. "What brings you out this way?"

The man in front, a burly fellow with a thick beard, glared at Morgan. "Ain't none of your concern. We're just paying a visit, that's all."

His hand dropped casually to rest on the butt of his revolver. The implication was clear. Morgan was outnumbered four to one.

His jaw tightened, but he kept his tone mild. "See, I can't let you do that. Unless you have a specific reason for visiting the orphanage, you need to ride on. These folks want to be left in peace." His hand drifted toward his hip. "I'm gonna have to ask you to turn around and ride out."

The bearded man sneered, his eyes narrowing in a dangerous glint. "Pretty bold talk for a lone deputy. You best get out of the way, less'n you want to get hurt."

His companions snickered. Morgan stood his ground, fingers brushing his holster.

"Last chance," he warned, holding the leader's gaze. "Ride on out, or there's gonna be trouble."

For a long, tense moment, no one moved. The air seemed to crackle with anticipation. Then, just as it seemed violence was inevitable, the bearded man released a menacing chuckle.

"Well, now, ain't you a brave one." He leaned over and spat in the dirt. "C'mon, boys. Reckon this pathetic orphanage ain't worth our time."

He wheeled his horse around, and the others followed. Morgan watched, hand still on the butt of his six-shooter, as they rode away, not relaxing his guard until they were out of sight.

He let out a slow breath, pulse still racing from the confrontation. Things could have gone bad real quick. At least the orphanage was safe—but for how long?

With a last look down the empty road, Morgan headed back to town, already dreading the next time those men came back this way.

Chapter Six

Morgan rode back to town, mulling over the confrontation with the gang of men. He'd have to let Gabe know about them and suggest a deputy spend time at the orphanage. He remembered how another group of men terrorized the orphanage the previous Christmas, going as far as to kidnap one of the children. Morgan sure didn't want to see a repeat of those bleak days.

Passing the saloon, he spotted a familiar figure leaning against the rail. Dutch looked up at the sound of hoofbeats and touched the brim of his hat in greeting.

"Morgan. Everything go all right at the orphanage?"

He swung down from the saddle. "Had a bit of excitement. Four men showed up when I was leaving. Scruffy, menacing. I asked their reason for stopping, and the leader told me it was none of my business. I was lucky they backed down and rode off. It could've gone either way."

Dutch's expression turned serious. "Tell me about them."

"Four men. Beards, mustaches. Smelled as if they hadn't bathed in months. The leader was a burly fella. He blustered some, but I stood my ground, and they rode off." Morgan shook his head. "I don't know what they were after, but I don't think we've seen the last of them."

"Hmm." Dutch rubbed his jaw. "Let's have a talk with Gabe. Do you remember the children I mentioned? The ones I delivered to the orphanage today?"

"Yeah."

"Their parents were gunned down by a group of men in Big Pine. That's why the children ran off. Could be the same men."

"I don't like where this is headed. Let's talk with Gabe before he leaves for home."

Dutch settled his hat down on his head. "Good idea. Let's go."

Morgan walked his horse up the street to outside the sheriff's office, tossing the reins over the post. Straightening his vest, he followed Dutch into the jail.

Inside, they found Gabe going through a stack of wanted posters at his desk. The sheriff looked up.

"Morgan. Dutch. Good to see you. What's going on?"

Morgan lowered himself into the chair across from Gabe's desk. He explained about Amelia spotting a group of men riding near the orphanage.

"She was pretty nervous about them. Four men

rode up as I was leaving the orphanage today. Mean looking bunch."

Gabe's expression darkened. He set down the posters in his hand. "They threaten you at all?"

"The leader acted tough but didn't draw on me. I told them if they didn't have specific business at the orphanage, they'd best be on their way."

"Do you think they'll be back?"

Morgan rubbed his jaw, recalling the ugly glares the men had given him. "I'd bet on it. They seemed real interested in the orphanage."

Gabe's brow furrowed. "That doesn't sound good. We need to find out who these men are and what they're doing here. I'll send a telegram to Sheriff Sterling in Big Pine, to see if he knows anything about them."

"It would be best if he could describe them. You might also ask if Wilma and Harry can identify the men who shot their parents," Dutch said.

Gabe nodded as he stood, grabbing his hat. "Good idea. With luck, Sterling will get back to me soon."

Morgan squinted against the bright sun as he shoved his hat down on his head the following morning. He walked the short distance to the jail, his thoughts focused on the strange encounter with the group of men. Who were they, and what was their reason for being at the orphanage?

Reaching the jail at the same time as Dutch, they headed inside.

Gabe looked up to face the two deputies. "Bernie just delivered this telegram." He held it up. "Take a look, Morgan."

Reading the description of the leader, he handed the paper back to Gabe.

"The description matches the man leading the gang I saw yesterday," Morgan said. "They have to be the same men who killed Wilma and Harry's parents. We need to do something before they hurt anyone at the orphanage."

"Agreed," Dutch chimed in. "We can't let them kill anyone else."

Gabe leaned forward. "There's something else." He held up a second telegram. "Sterling forgot to include this in the first telegram." He handed it to Dutch.

"I'll be. It says Wilma and Harry saw the shooting." He looked up. "Meaning those children can identify the killers. No wonder those men are trying to find them."

Gabe nodded. "All right. This is what we'll do."

Within the hour, Morgan and Dutch were riding toward the orphanage. Dismounting, they walked up the steps to the front door, their eyes scanning the trail behind them. Morgan was about to step inside when Dutch grabbed his arm.

"Look again."

Morgan did, spotting four riders emerging from a

growing cloud of dust. "I'd wager they're the same men. And they're riding fast."

"Agreed," Dutch said as Morgan opened the front door.

"Martha, we've got a problem," Morgan called out as they entered the house.

She rushed out of her office toward them. "What is it?"

"Did Amelia tell you about the group of men she's seen around here?"

"Yes. She told me last evening."

"There's a group of men riding toward us. This is just a guess, but Dutch and I believe they're the men who killed Wilma and Harry's parents. If so, there's a good chance the children can identify them."

Martha's face went white as a sheet. "What are they doing here?"

"We don't know yet," Dutch said. "Could be they're after Wilma and Harry."

She pulled back the curtain to look out the window. "They're almost here. I'd better get all the children into the basement. Are you going to tell them Wilma and Harry are here?"

"No," Morgan said. "We're going to try to find out what they want before making any decisions. We won't do anything to endanger the children."

With a terse nod, Martha rushed toward the classroom while Morgan and Dutch stepped outside. The riders were sitting atop their horses, not a friendly face among them. The hostile expressions indicated they were ready for a fight.

"Listen." Morgan held up a hand in a placating gesture. "We don't want trouble. We just need to know what you're doing here."

"None of your darned business," one of the men spat.

"Actually, it is our business," Dutch said. "You're wanted for murder, and we're here to take you in." The two deputies hovered their hands above the butt of their guns without drawing the weapons from the holsters. Any move could trigger a gunfight. It was a situation both wanted to avoid.

The outlaws shifted uneasily, their hands hovering near their guns. Morgan could feel his heart pounding in his chest, but he refused to show any fear.

"Look," Dutch said. "We don't want anyone to get hurt here. Come with us peacefully, and we'll make sure you get to Big Pine for a fair trial."

Morgan and Dutch stood their ground, their hands continuing to hover near their guns. They were outnumbered, but they weren't about to back down.

For a moment, it seemed the men might consider giving up. An intense silence grew until one of them made a slow move.

Morgan watched as the man's hand tightened around the grip of his gun. He knew the situation was about to turn ugly.

"All right, gentlemen. That's enough." A new voice cut through the tension.

Morgan turned to see Martha standing behind him, a shotgun aimed at the riders. Both hammers were cocked.

"Martha?" Morgan asked.

"I couldn't sit inside while there was a standoff happening outside." Her eyes flickered to the group of men.

"Get back inside, ma'am," Dutch said, his tone sharp. "It's not safe out here."

"Actually, I think it's safer out here than it is inside," she replied, her gaze steady.

For a moment, no one spoke, the tension thick in the air. Morgan could feel his heart pound in a painful beat.

"If you don't get yourselves out of here right now, I'm going to blow the fat man in the middle right off his horse." She pointed the shotgun at his chest. "If you think I won't, try something." Martha's hard voice had all the men looking at her.

"Listen, we don't want anyone to get hurt, or worse." Morgan's voice was calm, though resolute. "You need to come with us."

"I ain't going anywhere," one of the men growled, reaching for his gun.

Morgan acted fast, drawing his own gun and firing a warning shot over the man's head.

"That's enough." His eyes flashed in a final warning.

The men hesitated, exchanging glances before they drew their guns.

Before any of them could fire, Martha pulled the trigger, hitting the fat man square in the chest. The impact blew the outlaw into the air and off the back of his horse. The second shot hit another man in his right shoulder.

Morgan and Dutch dove for cover, aiming their six-shooters at the remaining two men.

Slamming their revolvers into holsters, the outlaws reined their horses around as Morgan and Dutch began firing. One toppled to the ground while the other guided his horse into the trees and disappeared.

Morgan and Dutch stood, their guns still smoking. Three men lay sprawled on the ground, dead or dying.

For a moment, Martha stood rigid, staring down at the men she'd shot. Lowering the shotgun, she gripped the edge of the doorpost, her face pale.

Morgan rushed to her, sliding his arm around her waist. "Let's get you inside, Martha."

She didn't resist as he guided her to one of the chairs, lowering her onto the seat. "Thank you, Morgan. I do believe I'll sit here for a bit. Will you and Deputy McFarlin move the bodies so the children won't see the carnage?"

"Yes, ma'am. We'll do that right now."

"Good."

For a moment, Morgan just stood there, staring down at her. He couldn't imagine what the woman had been thinking, though he was mighty glad she knew how to shoot.

Turning to look at Dutch, he could see a mix of emotions on his friend's face. Thankful for the outcome while surprised at how it had come about.

They both knew there was a chance the danger wasn't over. With one man getting away, they had to anticipate the threat hadn't ended.

"Come on," Dutch said, gesturing toward the outside. "We need to take care of the bodies and make sure everyone in the basement is all right."

Morgan began following him outside, then stopped. "I'll check on the men outside while you let Amelia and Rose know what happened. It'd be best if they kept the children where they are until we get those men out of sight."

"Understood. You might see how Martha's doing before going outside."

Morgan gave a short nod, leaning down. "Martha?"

Her eyes fluttered, then opened. Seconds ticked by before she remembered the events of the last half hour and sat up.

"We must check on the children."

"Dutch is doing that right now. We're going to keep them in the basement until we've taken care of the men outside."

"Yes, of course." When she started to stand, he placed a hand on her shoulder.

"Why don't you sit for a bit longer."

"No, no. I'm going to join the ladies and the children. Thank you for protecting everyone."

Morgan snorted a laugh. "Ma'am, you're the one who saved them and us. It was a fine thing you did out there, making sure those varmints stayed away from the children."

Helping her stand, he watched her walk to the stairs before he stepped outside. From the porch, he was certain at least two were dead. He wondered why they took a stand at an orphanage, and what or who inside cost them their lives.

Chapter Seven

Martha's eyes widened as she read the letter, her hand trembling. A business conglomerate out of Chicago was threatening legal action if the orphanage continued using water from their well. A well, the letter stated, which drew from a creek owned by the group of businessmen.

The letter had arrived from an attorney in Big Pine, stating it was their fourth attempt to resolve the issue. Yet this was the first time Martha knew of the dispute.

She hoped to resolve the water rights issue in an amicable manner, but the tone of the letter didn't sound promising. It implied the possible use of force to obtain the orphanage's compliance.

The orphanage couldn't survive without the water from their well. If it were to shut down, what would happen to the children?

Martha set her jaw, determined not to be bullied by an unseen group of men from across the country. Folding the letter, she informed Amelia and Rose she'd be leaving for town and wasn't sure when she'd return.

Outside, she swung into the saddle of her horse and began the ride to town. She intended to meet with the attorneys for the orphanage, Frannie Boudreaux and Griffin MacKenzie. They had to find a solution before the conglomerate made good on their threats.

Martha rode into Splendor, reining the horse to a halt outside the attorneys' office. Dismounting, she took a deep breath, straightened her shoulders, and strode inside.

"Mrs. Santori, what a pleasant surprise." Damon Broom, the legal secretary for Frannie and Griffin, rose from behind his desk. He was a sharp-eyed young man with youthful features and the soul of someone with much more experience. People underestimated him all the time. Most regretting their error. The same was the case for the two attorneys who employed Damon.

"What can we do for you?"

"I'm afraid this is not a social call. I must speak with Frannie or Griff at once."

"Of course. Please sit down and I'll see who's available." Damon returned a few minutes later with Frannie Boudreaux.

"It's good to see you, Martha. Please, come upstairs, and we'll discuss how I can help you."

Reaching the office, she didn't sit down before handing the letter to Frannie. The attorney scanned it, then read it again, her lips compressing into a thin line as she read.

"I see. This is most distressing."

"What can we do?" Martha asked.

The office door opened. Griffin MacKenzie entered. "Good morning, Martha."

"Hello, Griff." He looked at Frannie, taking the letter from her outstretched hand. His gray eyes darkened as he read the contents.

"Blast it all," Griffin muttered under his breath. "Have you received previous correspondence on this?"

"The letter you're holding is all I've received from this attorney in Big Pine."

"It doesn't surprise me. Fortune hunters have been using this ploy for a while. Though, this one implies threats beyond legal action."

"I'm worried about the children. There must be some solution," Martha said urgently. "The orphanage needs water. Without it..." She trailed off, worry creasing her brow.

Frannie and Griffin exchanged glances. "It will take some time," Frannie said. "Many of the groups have deep pockets and slick lawyers."

Griffin leaned against the desk, arms crossed over his broad chest. "We'll fight them with every legal avenue we have. First, we must ascertain if their claim has any merit. The letter gives us what we need to check through the land office. I recommend we start there."

"I'll do whatever it takes." Martha's voice held a vehemence seldom heard.

"It could get ugly," Griffin warned.

She lifted her chin. "I will not be intimidated. The children are my priority."

Frannie nodded, her voice as steely as Martha's. "Good. Then here is what I propose…"

The three huddled together, voices low and urgent as they strategized. After an hour, they had the kernel of a plan.

"I'll send Damon to the land office right away. Depending on what he finds, we'll ride for Big Pine at first light the day after tomorrow," Griffin said. "I know their lawyer. He's slick as an eel and doesn't mind twisting the law to suit his client's purpose. Even so, we may be able to reason with him."

Martha sat relaxed in the saddle as she, her husband, Deputy Cole Santori, and Griffin rode across the rugged landscape toward Big Pine. Thinking of her comfort, Cole had suggested taking a wagon, acknowledging it would slow their pace. Insisting time was critical, Martha urged them to ride horses.

The endless scrub fell around them beneath the simmering sun. Cole kept casting her sideways glances, as if worried she'd topple from her horse at any moment. She kept her gaze fixed ahead. There was too much at stake to show any weakness now.

After hours of riding, they arrived in Big Pine.

Martha removed her hat, smoothing her hair and dress in an attempt to compose herself before entering the lawyer's office.

The meeting was tense from the outset. The lawyer, a polished man named Leonard Barstow, regarded them with an icy gaze from the other side of his desk.

"I believe my clients were quite clear regarding their position on the water rights," Barstow said.

"The orphanage has depended on that water since we opened," Martha argued. "You cannot simply take it from children in need."

"Your problems are not ours, madam. My clients have a legal claim to the water."

Martha felt her temper rising. "And I'm telling you, sir, we will fight your clients' claim with every resource available. Your clients are attempting to steal water."

"Are you threatening me, Mrs. Santori?" Barstow's mild tone belied the anger within.

"I do not make threats, sir," Martha replied. "Only promises."

They glared at each other across the desk. Martha could feel Griffin and Cole tense beside her.

"As you can see from the documents provided, a final sale was never consummated by your clients," Griffin said. "We have a strong cause for legal action if your clients continue with their false claim." He didn't add that Martha had submitted a bid to Horace Clausen to buy the adjoining property. Or the fact Griffin had obtained a binding agreement from neighboring ranches stating the orphanage had use of the water in perpetuity.

"And if you try to intimidate or threaten my wife, her employees, or the children at the orphanage in any way, you'll regret those attempts," Cole said.

After a moment, Barstow leaned back in his chair. "I will convey your concerns to my clients. I would warn you not to get your hopes up."

"When shall we expect their reply?" Griffin asked.

"A day, maybe longer. I assume you'll be staying overnight in Big Pine."

"Yes. We'll be at the Imperial Hotel. I'll expect to hear from you before we leave town." Griffin didn't offer his hand as he stood.

Jaw clenched, Martha rose. "This isn't over, Mr. Barstow." Gathering her skirts, she swept from the office, Cole and Griffin on her heels.

Martha's mind churned with plans and contingencies, but an undercurrent of fear ran beneath it all.

Morgan hauled another small bed into the crowded dormitory room, a large room created from two smaller ones. Amelia was busy making up the small beds with blankets and sheets while Rose swept the floor.

"There, in the corner," Rose said.

Morgan set it down and stepped back, wiping his brow. The room was now filled with two rows of beds, leaving the tiniest amount of space to walk between them.

"I think that's all we can fit," he said. In the past few weeks, more children had arrived, overflowing the orphanage's capacity.

Amelia tucked the sheet corners neatly. "I don't know how we'll manage to feed and care for them all."

Morgan put a comforting hand on her shoulder. "We'll find a way," he said. Amelia gave him a tired smile.

"At least the dormitory and classroom have been expanded," Rose said. "We're bursting at the seams everywhere else."

They left the crowded dormitory and headed downstairs, on a mission to check food supplies. Amelia kept a detailed list of what they had on hand and what was needed. She grabbed it from a hook near the sink.

"Flour, salt, sugar, and lard are all fine. Enough for more than a month. We're low on dried beans, peas, cornmeal, dried fruit, molasses, and coffee. Stan Petermann will extend our credit, but I don't know for how long."

"Don't fret about it, Amelia. Martha will talk to him when she gets back," Rose said.

"I know."

"It's the water," Morgan said.

Amelia nodded. "What if those businessmen take

it away?"

He smiled, placing a hand on her shoulder. "The town won't let that happen."

Despite the circumstances, Morgan felt certain between the townsfolk and donations from back east, they'd keep the orphanage alive.

Martha, Cole, and Griffin returned to Splendor exhausted after three tense days away. Martha's face was drawn, her shoulders slumped with fatigue. Cole guided their horses to the livery, his movements slow and weary.

Griffin dismounted stiffly, rubbing his lower back. "I'm too old to spend that many hours in the saddle," he complained.

Martha said nothing, her thoughts clearly elsewhere. Griffin had argued passionately for the orphanage's rights, citing the facts Damon had obtained from the land office. The businessmen hadn't followed the requirements for closing their purchase of the land. Even if they had, Griffin had told Barstow the orphanage land included rights to the creek. By the time the conglomerate made a decision on how to proceed, Martha Santori would be the owner of the adjoining parcel.

The conglomerate's lawyer had been intractable. Still, Martha and the orphanage had the law on their side, and a town full of people willing to fight for what was right.

The only time Barstow flinched was when Griffin brought up the names of people in Splendor who'd moved from back east. Mentioning the Evans family made a noticeable impression.

Cole met her eyes, understanding her determination despite her obvious exhaustion. "You should get some rest. We'll meet with Griff again in the morning."

"What about you?"

Bending down, he kissed her. "I'm going to let Gabe know what happened in Big Pine, then I'll be home."

Martha nodded, though she knew sleep would prove elusive with so much at stake. As she walked the short distance to their house, the weight of the orphans' fate pressed heavily on her shoulders.

Chapter Eight

Martha gathered Amelia and Rose in the small parlor room the next morning. Gabe had sent Morgan to the orphanage early, hoping his presence would ease their worry. He joined the group.

Martha had dark circles under her eyes from a sleepless night, but her gaze was sharp and focused.

"The negotiations did not go as well as we hoped," she began without preamble. "The conglomerate's lawyer refuses to budge on the water rights issue. Our lawyers believe their move to seize the rights is nothing but bluster. They assume we're illiterate and without the means to fight them. They're wrong on both counts."

The women exchanged hopeful glances.

"What can they do to stop us from using the water before this gets resolved?" Amelia asked.

Martha clenched her hand on top of her desk. "They could petition the judge for an injunction, which would legally bar us from accessing the creek until the case is settled. Griff told me a resolution could take months, though he believes he can speed the process because of the children."

"I hope he's right." Rose voiced what they were all thinking.

"There must be something we can do," Morgan said. He felt a fierce surge of protectiveness for the women and children.

Martha shook her head. "According to Griffin, legally, our hands are tied. We'll keep pressing the judge. However, Griff, Frannie, and I are making alternative provisions for water."

"What provisions?" Morgan asked.

"The conglomerate attempted to buy the neighboring land. They failed to complete the purchase. I have given Horace Clausen my bid to purchase. He's promised to let me know within a few days if I can go forward with buying the land."

"If it doesn't go through?" he asked.

Martha shrugged, though her eyes blazed with defiance. "Then we'd need to drill another well."

The room was silent, Amelia and Rose contemplating the terrible possibility of the orphanage closing.

Just then, a knock sounded urgently at the front door. Amelia hurried to answer it, returning a moment later with a piece of paper in her hand.

"Bernie Griggs rode out with a telegram for you."

Martha took it with a frown, reading the contents. As understanding dawned, her eyes widened. She looked up, a spark of hope chasing away the fatigue in her expression.

"It's from Griff. It seems the water rights issue may resolve itself after all," she said. "However, we do have another issue and there's little time." She refolded the telegram, her jaw set with determination. "We need to leave for the creek at once."

Amelia, Rose, and Morgan stared at her, perplexed.

Martha hurried out the front door of the orphanage, the telegram clutched tightly in her hand. She continued running, the others following close behind, curiosity and anticipation propelling their steps toward the creek.

"The creek, you said?" Amelia fell into pace beside Martha. "What's happened?"

"They're attempting to divert the water." Martha stopped to speak with all three of them. "The conglomerate has stationed men upriver to divert the creek before it can reach the orphanage lands."

Morgan's expression darkened. "Sabotage. They're trying to force you into compliance."

Martha nodded, her lips pressed into a thin line. "Which is why we must get there straight away, before..."

She broke off as a rumble sounded in the distance. They paused, gazing uphill where the creek cut through a copse of trees.

Martha paled. "No," she whispered. "It may already be too late."

Like a living thing, the water slithered and slid over rocks and fallen logs, seeking paths back to its original channel. But the new obstruction held fast, diverting the flow away from orphanage land.

For a long moment, the group stood frozen, watching the water make a dramatic turn to the west. Then Cole rode up, dismounted, and slid his arms around Martha.

"Wagons and more men are coming, sweetheart. We'll haul off as many smaller rocks as we can, and attempt to move the larger boulders. At least some water will get through."

Everyone shook off their stunned disbelief and scrambled into action. As they hurried for tools to move the obstruction, Martha put a hand on Cole's arm.

"Thank you."

He nodded, his eyes gentle despite the set of his jaw.

Martha's mind raced as she watched the creek divert from its normal path. They had to act fast before the flow was completely blocked.

"I'm going to ride into town and gather as many volunteers as possible," Morgan said. "We'll need all the help we can get to move those boulders."

Cole nodded. "I'm going to lead the wagons to the diversion." Mounting, he rode off.

Martha hurried to the orphanage, Rose right behind her, where several older boys were resting after morning chores.

"We need your help. Gather ropes, pry bars, anything we can use as levers. Meet me at the creek."

The boys, along with some of the older girls, jumped into action, sensing the urgency in Martha's voice. She turned to Rose.

"Keep the younger ones inside. I need to harness the horses and drive our wagon to the creek."

Rose's eyes widened, nodding. "Don't worry about the children, Martha. I'll take good care of them."

At the creek, Martha surveyed the obstruction, her jaw tightening. The stream's flow had slowed to a trickle. They had no time to lose.

Soon, volunteers were arriving, Morgan leading a determined group from town. Horses strained against the boulders as men heaved on ropes and beams. Rock by rock, they battled to clear a path for the water.

Morgan threw his weight against a pry bar, unflinching when the rock began to move. He knew none of the volunteers would give in to the men who sought to destroy the town's orphanage to satisfy their own greed.

"What can I do?" Dutch McFarlin stood beside him, a crowbar in his hand.

"We'll need several men to move those larger boulders. Can you help gather and direct them?"

"Sure can, but I doubt they'll need much directing." Dutch took off toward a group of people watching from up the hill.

Everyone helped in whatever way they could. Even young children carried the smaller rocks to the wagons, wiping hands down their pants and dresses before running back for more.

Amelia took a break, swiping a hand across her forehead, her gaze landing on Morgan. No matter the time of day or circumstances, her heart gave a twist each time their eyes met.

She'd never been courted in New York. It was one reason she'd joined Rachel Pelleteir's other friends on the trip west. Watching Morgan, she wondered if he might be thinking about spending more time with her. She hoped so.

Chuckling at the foolish thoughts, she bent down, lifting a large rock and rolling it in the opposite direction. She didn't worry about preparing meals, the level of supplies, or anything other than reclaiming the precious water.

Martha wiped her brow, glancing upstream as the last boulder shifted. Water began flowing again, the creek gurgling back to life.

Cheers went up from the volunteers. Cole clasped shoulders, praising their efforts.

Martha noticed Griffin standing apart, his expression grim. She went to him.

"We've won this battle. Yet you don't seem relieved."

Griffin shook his head. "This is only the opening salvo. I've no doubt there will be more to come."

Martha's mouth thinned. She knew he was right. The men trying to steal the water wouldn't accept defeat. Those kinds of men never did.

"Then we'll be ready," she said. "Whatever they do next, we'll be ready."

Griffin searched her face, then nodded. If anyone could rally this town, it was the woman before him.

Martha and Griffin walked back to join the others, determination in their strides. Cole gave his wife a questioning look, but she just shook her head. They would talk later.

For now, the mood was celebratory. Men laughed and clapped each other on the back as the stream flowed freely again. The children from the orphanage had been brought out to see the efforts to save their water source, cheering and clapping.

"We did it!" Amy, one of the youngest orphans cried, jumping up and down. Martha smiled and ruffled her hair.

"For now, yes. But we must remain vigilant."

The little girl's face fell. "You mean the bad men might come back?"

Martha crouched down to look her in the eyes. "They might try, but remember, we are strong together. As long as we stand united, no one can defeat us."

The girl nodded, reassured. Martha gave her a quick hug before standing. There was still much to be done, but this battle was won.

Cole approached, his expression serious. "We've got riders coming. Could be more trouble brewing."

Martha tensed. "Then let's go find out what fresh chaos awaits us now." She straightened her shoulders.

As they walked up the hill to meet the three riders, women and men joined them, resolve etched on their features. Near the top, Gabe, Nick Barnett, and Noah, plus several others, stood facing the men on horseback. Griffin, Cole, and Morgan joined them.

"Leonard Barstow is in the lead," Griffin said. "I wonder why he came all the way from Big Pine."

Cole crossed his arms. "Perhaps so he could report back to his clients the water rights issue was over. The man's a snake, Griff."

"What's so darned puzzling is he knows his clients are in the wrong." Griffin took a step forward.

When the riders approached, Gabe introduced himself. "I'm the sheriff. What's your business here?"

"Leonard Barstow, from Big Pine." He leaned over the saddlehorn, surveying what the town had accomplished. He glanced at Griffin and Cole before addressing Gabe.

"First, I want you to know I had no part in diverting the water. Someone in Chicago directed those actions. My associates and I rode in this morning about another matter. We heard what happened, and what you and the townsfolk were doing. Impressive."

Gabe's fisted hands rested on his hips. "You let your clients know whatever they have planned, we'll be standing in their way."

"They are no longer my clients. The instant I heard what transpired, I sent a telegram, ending our relationship." Barstow looked at Griffin. "If anything more happens, you can count on me to help you and the town."

Griffin gave a slight nod.

"I should get back. My associates and I have a supper meeting at the Eagle's Nest. I've heard it's a fine place, Sheriff Evans."

As Gabe and Barstow concluded their discussion, Cole turned to Griffin.

"If anything more does happen, are you going to seek help from Barstow?"

Snickering, Griffin shook his head. "Not in this lifetime. Slime runs pretty deep in the men who've got it."

Chapter Nine

Morgan hammered a new railing onto the orphanage's front porch, his back and arms glistening from the intense heat. Though the creek had been cleared and the water flowed freely again, there was still much work to be done prior to the first snows in the fall.

As Morgan worked, he glanced at the children playing in the yard. Their laughter and smiles couldn't help but lift the spirits of even the darkest soul. This place had become a second home to him.

"Need a hand with that?" a familiar voice called out.

Morgan turned to see Dutch walking up, toolbox in hand.

"Sure, grab a hammer," Morgan replied.

The two worked side by side, making steady progress on the repairs. Dutch whistled an upbeat tune as he reinforced the porch steps. Though different in temperament, their shared commitment to the orphanage had forged an unexpected bond between them.

After securing the final railing, Morgan sat on the top step and wiped his brow. Dutch joined him, both men admiring their handiwork.

"Those stairs weren't going to last much longer," Dutch remarked. "It's a good thing we got to them when we did."

"This place needs a lot of work. Those kids deserve a safe home."

"That, they do," Dutch agreed. He studied his friend's face. "You really care about this place, don't you?"

Morgan thought for a moment before replying. "I never had much growing up. My family struggled. If it hadn't been for the kindness of others, I don't know where I'd be today." He glanced at the children playing in the large yard.

Dutch stretched out his legs as their gazes moved over the trees in the distance. Ever since one of the four outlaws had gotten away a week earlier, everyone had been more vigilant, expecting the remaining man to return.

The two sat in companionable silence, enjoying the sunshine and sounds of the children. There were always jobs to be done, but it was work they enjoyed doing.

Morgan listened to the children's laughter, feeling content. His thoughts turned to Amelia, the orphanage's cook. He'd come to admire her dedication to the children and her strength of spirit. Though their interactions had been limited to the orphanage, he felt a growing connection with her.

Glancing at his pocket watch, Morgan stood. "I'm going to ask Miss Amelia if she'd join me for a picnic by the creek this weekend." *While I have the courage to do it,* he didn't add.

Dutch grinned and gave Morgan a playful nudge. "She seems like a fine woman. Good luck."

He stepped inside, wiping his boots on the rug while listening to soft humming coming from the kitchen. He knew she rose at five each morning to start breakfast for the growing number of children. After breakfast, she started preparing lunch. The process was repeated for supper. Her breaks consisted of helping Rose in the classroom and tidying the enlarged dormitory, where the children slept.

Morgan waited for a few minutes, gathering his courage before walking into the kitchen. He found her drying breakfast dishes and stacking them on a shelf. He cleared his throat.

Amelia spun around, almost dropping a plate. "Morgan...you startled me. Have you come in for coffee or water? I don't have much else right now." Her mouth had twisted into a grin.

"Nothing right now, thank you. Amelia, I was wondering if you'd do me the honor of joining me for a picnic this Sunday after church? Nothing fancy and not far from town."

Her face lit up. "Why, I'd love to, Morgan. A picnic sounds delightful." She smiled, her eyes twinkling.

His heart lifted. "Wonderful. I'll fetch a wagon and meet you after morning service, if that's all right?"

Amelia nodded. "Perfect. I'll look forward to our outing."

Morgan sat on the wagon seat, more nervous than at any other time in his life. He'd worn his best shirt and pants, shined his boots, and brushed his hat.

Spotting him, Amelia rushed to the wagon and climbed up before he could help her. Sitting beside him, she arranged her skirt.

The smile she flashed him almost knocked him backward off the wagon seat. "It's a gorgeous day for a picnic, don't you think?"

"Uh...yes, it is. I...uh, packed some sandwiches, apples, and molasses cookies from the boardinghouse," Morgan said, slapping the reins to get the horses moving.

"Perfect." She gazed at the shops and houses rolling by as they made their way out of town.

Soon, they passed the last buildings and were surrounded by open fields and rolling hills. Aspen trees waved in the breeze, and birds fluttered and chirped.

Morgan drove them to a shady spot by Wildfire Creek, hopping down to help Amelia from the wagon. He spread out a blanket and unpacked the food, pouring them each a cup of cool water from his canteen.

"Hope this is all right." Morgan helped her onto the blanket, taking a place next to her.

Seeing the concern on his face, she placed a hand on his arm. "This is wonderful." She grabbed a sandwich, unwrapped it, and took a bite. "Excellent." She smiled.

They took their time, chatting about the orphanage and sharing funny stories of the children's antics. Amelia laughed freely, feeling comfortable with Morgan.

When they finished their meal, Morgan lay back on the blanket, hands laced behind his head. "You know, I never thanked you for asking if I'd be interested in volunteering. The work has made a world of difference to me, and I hope for the orphanage."

Amelia smiled. "What you've done has made a great difference. I'm just glad I suggested you speak with Martha. This place is special to all of us." She paused. "The children have given me purpose. My life in New York was so frivolous, so empty. I was merely a decoration, an accessory for my family's social ambitions."

She looked down, fingering the edge of her skirt. "As the youngest, my mother doted on me, but, I don't know...didn't really see me. My father only valued my ability to make a profitable match. I felt invisible."

Morgan studied her face, noticing past wounds in the sadness in her eyes. He also saw the strength she'd gained living in Splendor.

"I'm sorry, Amelia. I know the children see you, as do I. Strong and capable."

"Thank you, Morgan. That means a lot."

They held each other's gaze a moment, until a hawk cried overhead, circling in the vibrant blue sky. The interruption broke the spell of the moment.

"Tell me about where you grew up," Amelia said.

"Not much to tell. I'm the middle of three brothers, plus two younger sisters. Our mother died giving birth to our youngest sister. Pop died a few years ago, leaving my oldest brother and me to raise the others and run the farm. By the time I was seventeen, it seemed certain we'd lose the farm unless something happened. It was decided I'd try to find work and send money home."

"So you left the farm?"

"Yes. I joined the Union Army, and met Tucker and Jonas right away. We've been friends ever since."

"You've been sending money home all this time?"

"Every time I get paid." He shook his head. "It's not enough, though. I just don't know what else to do. I make decent money as a deputy, and don't have many other skills. Not that would pay more than what I make now."

"Your siblings will have to come up with some additional ideas. You can't be expected to support all four of them."

"The farm never made us any money. With seven people in the family, we grew enough to eat, and our two cows provided milk, butter, and cheese. Pa always had cattle to butcher. Ma sold jams and canned vegetables in town at the general store. She used the money to buy flour, sugar, salt, and cornmeal." He swallowed, taking a deep breath.

"Do you miss them?"

He nodded. "Not as much as I used to. The job, my friends, and work at the orphanage all keep me busy. There are days I get up at sunrise and lay down near midnight."

"Long hours," she said.

He shrugged. "I don't mind."

Morgan cleared his throat and sat up, sensing the conversation shifting to something more serious.

"I should tell you about some concerning reports Gabe's received. Seems a band of outlaws have been hitting settlers and travelers between Laramie and Big Pine. Robbing farms, rustling cattle, stopping stagecoaches. They're a vicious bunch, by all accounts."

Amelia's brow furrowed with worry. "How awful. Do you think they'll come this way?"

Morgan shook his head. "I doubt it. Splendor's too big for them to try anything here. I wanted you to know, just in case. I'll talk to Martha when I'm at the orphanage tomorrow."

He placed a reassuring hand on her shoulder. "Gabe is deciding what to do. He's been through this many times since moving to Splendor. I'm almost certain he'll select one or two deputies to watch the orphanage. We already patrol the road between town and the orphanage. You and the others will be safe."

Amelia nodded, comforted by his solid presence. Still, a shiver went through her.

"We should go over emergency plans at the orphanage," Morgan continued. "Make sure you, Martha, and Rose know how to handle a rifle and six-shooter, just in case."

"You really believe that's necessary?"

"I do. Handling a firearm is a good skill to have for a man or woman."

"Of course," Amelia agreed. She imagined Martha approving such training for their protection. "I think Martha took training from Gabe and Sean MacLaren, and some deputies last summer."

He remembered how Martha shot the men outside the orphanage. "I believe you're right."

Morgan drove Amelia back to the orphanage before returning the wagon to Noah. As he left the livery, Gabe rode up, his face grim.

"Morgan. I just got word from Moosejaw, a settlement east of Big Pine. It was hit hard by the band of outlaws. Took livestock, food stores, killed two men."

Morgan clenched his jaw. The settlement was a good forty miles east of Splendor.

"So far, we're safe. Sheriff Parker Sterling will let me know if they hit Big Pine," Gabe said. "I'm going to post a few of the deputies to keep watch. I want you out at the orphanage."

Morgan nodded. "I'll head out there first thing tomorrow."

"Plan to stay there until I tell you otherwise."

"Yes, sir. I'll keep watch."

Gabe gave a crisp nod before wheeling his horse around, galloping toward the jail.

Chapter Ten

Morgan spent the next few days stationed at the orphanage, keeping a close watch over the children and grounds. Though he maintained a cheerful demeanor, he was troubled.

Gabe had sent word the bandit gang had hit a stagecoach traveling between Moosejaw and Big Pine. They were getting bolder, and Morgan feared what could happen if they continued moving west.

One morning, as Morgan was chopping firewood, Martha Santori approached him. The stately woman who helped run the orphanage had a serious look on her face.

"Morgan," she began without preamble. "I'd like to request your assistance in an important matter."

He lowered his axe. "Of course, Martha. What can I do?"

"I want you to train Amelia, Rose, and some of our older children in the use of firearms. I know it's unusual, but these are dangerous times. If those devils attack, the children must be able to defend themselves."

"I was going to bring up the same. We can start tomorrow."

Martha exhaled in relief. "Thank you. I'll let Amelia and Rose know. We'll select which children to include."

"Fine with me. I'll ride to town and get a few more weapons and ammunition. I won't be gone long."

He took the wagon to the jail, found Gabe, and explained Martha's request. "I have no issue with training them."

"It's a good idea. I'm going to ask Tucker to go with you. What do you need?"

Morgan explained, then went off to find Tucker. After saddling his horse, Tucker helped Morgan load the guns and ammunition into the wagon.

Tying his horse to the back of the wagon, Tucker sat next to Morgan as they rode to the orphanage.

"Whose idea was this? Not that I think it's bad to make sure they know how to handle a shotgun and revolver."

"It was something I planned to bring up with Martha. She surprised me. Brought it up before I had the chance. We'll start tomorrow morning."

After breakfast, Morgan and Tucker stood before a line of solemn young faces, including Amelia and

Rose. The men had laid out an array of revolvers and shotguns.

"All right," Morgan said. "This is serious business. Tucker and I are going to teach you how to handle these safely and take aim properly."

He glanced toward the play yard and smiled. The younger children stood in a group behind them, watching and listening.

Morgan demonstrated loading, cocking, and firing the weapons toward targets he and Tucker had set up. Then the men let each person handle the guns, one by one, guiding their stance and grip.

Soon, Morgan divided the group in half. His group included Amelia, while Tucker's included Rose. Morgan had seen how his friend watched Rose each time he visited the orphanage or spotted her in town. The orphanage teacher intrigued Tucker, the same as Amelia intrigued him. Maybe today's lesson would push Tucker to make a move.

The shots rang out as the men supervised the training with a keen eye. The students were eager, doing their best to hold the weapons, aim, and fire as directed. The group did better than either Morgan or Tucker expected. One girl had trouble seeing the targets, doing fine when they had her close the distance by a few yards.

By day's end, the students had begun learning valuable skills to protect themselves and each other against any potential threat.

Morgan and Tucker surveyed the group of deter-mined young faces gathered before them. Their eyes shone with courage and resolve.

They felt a swell of pride for these orphan boys and girls who'd already endured so much hardship. Now they stood eager to learn skills to protect themselves and the little ones.

Morgan cleared his throat. "You've all done real fine today. But the training isn't over. Shooting still targets is one thing. Defending lives is another."

The children nodded solemnly.

"So, tomorrow, we'll be moving on to new drills," Morgan continued. "Learning to load fast, take cover, and watch all directions at once."

He turned to Amelia and Rose. "You ladies did real well, too. I'd recommend you get some rest tonight. You'll be helping Tucker and me run drills with the boys and girls tomorrow."

"We'll be ready," Amelia said. Beside her, Rose's chin lifted in determination.

Morgan gave them an approving nod. Then his gaze swept over the group.

The children stood before them, spines straight, jaws set. At this moment, they were no longer lost, no longer afraid. They were becoming fighters. Protectors.

Morgan and Tucker showed the students how to clean their weapons, before dismissing them to rest up for tomorrow's training. As they filed out of the yard, chattering excitedly, he and Tucker glanced at each other, feeling a swell of pride.

They were gathering the targets when Amelia approached. "That was wonderful how you motivated them," she said. "They look up to both of you."

Morgan rubbed his neck, abashed. "Thank you, Amelia."

"It's more than that." She smiled at them. "You've given them confidence and purpose. They feel strong now instead of scared. Like they can handle anything."

Morgan shrugged, but her praise lit a little glow inside him. He cared about these kids. Wanted them to thrive.

"Of course, the shooting lessons help, too," Amelia added with a twinkle in her eyes. "Soon, we'll have the best sharpshooters in the territory."

The men chuckled before Tucker excused himself to start storing the guns away for tomorrow. And, Morgan suspected, look for Rose.

"As long as they remember what we taught them about safety and discipline, we'll be happy."

They stood smiling at each other as the sun began to disappear behind the orphanage. Morgan thought Amelia looked especially pretty with the glow lighting up her face.

"Well, I better help Tucker pack away the guns for the night. We'll start again tomorrow after breakfast."

"Of course. And I should check on supper." Amelia touched his arm lightly. "Thank you again, Morgan. For everything."

He nodded, throat feeling tight. Tipping his hat, he strode off.

Morgan's boots crunched on the dry earth as he walked the perimeter of the orphanage grounds after supper. He kept his senses alert, a shotgun in one hand, as he scanned the tree line for any signs of disturbance. All was quiet.

Turning the corner, he spotted Amelia sitting on the porch steps, gazing out at the darkening landscape. She turned when she heard his approach, giving him a little wave.

"Hey, there," Morgan said, leaning against the railing. "Are they all tucked in for the night?"

"Just about." Amelia nodded through the open front door. "Tucker volunteered to help Rose get things under control. She insisted I take a break."

Morgan chuckled. "You work mighty hard around here." His friend's laughter wafted outside through the open door. "I'm glad Tucker is keeping busy."

"He and Rose seem to be getting along well."

"Yes, they do."

She studied him with a little furrow between her brows. "Are you sure you don't need some help on watch? I don't mind keeping you company."

Morgan felt a surge of warmth at her concern. "That's all right. Don't want you losing sleep on my account."

"I don't mind..." She hesitated. "To be honest, I feel safer knowing you're close by."

Morgan met her earnest gaze, something powerful passing between them. Clearing his throat, he glanced away. "Tucker and I will take turns. We've got things covered."

"I know you do." Her voice was soft. She stood then, smoothing out her skirt. "Well, I should let you get back to it. Goodnight, Morgan."

"'Night, Amelia." He watched until she stepped inside before resuming his patrol.

Morgan circled the perimeter of the orphanage, alert and watchful. The moon was bright, illuminating the surrounding land. Even the wind was still, creating an eerie quiet.

As he reached the back of the property, a flicker of movement caught his eye. Morgan tensed, raising his shotgun. Narrowing his gaze into the darkness, he spotted a shadowy figure slipping through the brush toward the orphanage.

With swift silence, Morgan pursued, his hands tightening on the gun. As he closed in, the moonlight revealed a rough-looking man in dirty clothes. Could he be one of the bandits they'd been warned about?

Morgan cocked his gun. "Hold it right there."

The man froze, then turned with a snarl, his own pistol raised. A tense beat passed. Morgan kept his aim steady. "Drop it. Now."

With a growled curse, the man lowered his weapon. Morgan approached warily, disarming him.

"What are you doing skulking around here at night?"

He got his answer when the man spat on the

ground.

"You picked the wrong place to rob," Morgan said, binding the man's hands. "The sheriff will deal with you soon enough."

Marching the culprit to the front of the orphanage, Morgan rapped on the door. He could hear boots pounding on the wood floor before Tucker opened the door, startled to see the captive.

"Who do you have, Morgan?"

"He's not talking, so I assume he must be one of the bandits. I need to take him to the jail."

"Not tonight," Tucker said. "If you're right, others could be hiding in the trees, waiting for one of us to ride off."

Morgan knew he was right. "I'll put him in the basement, and cinch him up to a support post for the night."

"I can ride him into town before breakfast," Tucker offered.

The sound of horse hooves pounding toward them had them drawing their weapons. As the rider came into sight, both relaxed.

"Cole. Didn't know you were riding out tonight," Morgan said.

"I'm tired of my bride sleeping here and me in town." Cole dismounted and climbed up the steps. "Who's this?"

"Caught him creeping around outside. I'm going to tie him up in the basement. I'll take him to the jail tomorrow." Morgan shoved the man into the house.

"I'll help you." Tucker followed him inside as Martha stepped out of her office.

"What's going on?"

"Everything's fine, ma'am," Tucker assured her. "But let Miss Amelia know she was right to feel uneasy. Morgan caught a man prowling around outside. We're tying him up in the basement for the night. Oh, and Cole rode in. He's outside."

"Cole?" Martha hurried to find her husband, rushing into his arms. "What are you doing here?"

"We've got to figure something out, sweetheart. I'm tired of sleeping alone." He bent his head to kiss her.

Chapter Eleven

Morgan rode into town early the next morning. Behind him, he ponied the prisoner's horse. The prisoner, whom Morgan and Tucker had dubbed Jonesy, was tied securely to the saddle.

Riding through town, he stopped at the jail, releasing the straps holding Jonesy to the saddle, and pulled him to the ground.

Gripping Jonesy's bound wrists, he marched him into the jail. Jonesy's eyes were downcast, his face an impassive mask despite the indignity of his situation. Morgan's expression was stern, his jaw set as he focused on delivering the captive to one of the cells in the back of the jail.

Gabe stood from where he worked at his desk, grabbed the ring of keys, and opened one of the cell doors. As soon as Morgan shoved Jonesy inside, Gabe locked the door.

"All right, Jonesy. You're gonna tell me everything you know about the bandits."

The prisoner glared at Gabe through the bars. "I

already told the deputy," he nodded at Morgan, "I don't know nothin'."

A corner of Gabe's mouth tilted upward. "We know you know more than you're sharing. Give us the names of your accomplices, or you'll be spending a long time at Deer Lodge."

Jonesy's eyes flashed before a sneer twisted his mouth. "Go ahead and lock me up. I ain't talking." He spat on the floor in contempt.

Gabe shrugged. "Fine, have it your way."

He walked back to his desk, Morgan taking one more look at Jonesy before joining his boss. Once they were out of earshot, he spoke up.

"I don't think he's going to talk. He seems loyal to his gang." Morgan sat down across from Gabe. "I'm not sure he's even part of the gang you heard about."

Tossing the keys in a drawer, Gabe's face remained impassive. "He wasn't watching the orphanage by himself. He's part of some outfit. Whether it's the one from Laramie or not is what we need to find out."

Morgan nodded. As a deputy, he felt the same burden of responsibility to determine the reason Jonesy stalked the orphanage.

"There's got to be some way we can get him to talk," Morgan mused.

Gabe lowered his voice. "We could let rumors spread he betrayed the gang, and hope word gets back to them. He'll realize his only protection is right here."

Morgan frowned. "It's a long shot. No one knows

where to find the bandits."

"True. I'll speed it up by sending telegrams to Sheriff Sterling in Big Pine and the sheriffs of Moosejaw, Red Dog, and Laramie, in case they ride south."

Morgan knew they had few options. "What can I do?"

"Stay at the orphanage." Gabe shifted in his chair. "Since opening, it has had more than a reasonable share of problems. The outlaw gang last summer, last year's flood, the diversion of the creek, the bandits shot last week, and now this. I don't understand why an orphanage has become a target."

"I've wondered the same. Could any of them be connected?"

"It's possible the creek diversion is connected with Jonesy. If he's working alone, he might've been ordered to taint the well."

Morgan's brows shot up. "You think so?"

"It wouldn't surprise me. You and Tucker are to stay out there until we discover if Jonesy is on his own, or if he's connected to the bandits from Laramie."

"Or the conglomerate who wants to control the water." Morgan stood.

"Be vigilant. Let me know if anything suspicious happens."

"Sure will. I best get moving. I'm expected back at the orphanage soon," he said.

Morgan straightened his hat against the intense morning sun and stepped outside. He blinked a few times, letting his eyes adjust, before making his way to his chestnut gelding.

Swinging into the saddle, he grabbed the line to Jonesy's horse. He rode toward the livery, intending to leave it with Noah, then changed his mind. Until they sorted out Jonesy, he saw no reason they couldn't use the horse at the orphanage.

He nudged the gelding's flanks, guiding him out of town. The clop of hooves accompanied his reflections about the prisoner. He hoped Gabe's plan worked, for all their sakes. Something in his gut told him there was more to this Jonesy character than he'd first thought.

The ride to the orphanage was a short one, giving Morgan little time to wrestle with his doubts. He'd have to trust Gabe on this. The sheriff had gotten them out of worse scrapes since Morgan had signed on as a deputy.

Morgan pushed his concerns aside. Right now, he needed to tell Tucker what he and Gabe had discussed. Anything else would have to wait.

Dutch tipped his hat to a local couple as he exited the jailhouse. Gabe had given him simple instructions to spread the word about Jonesy talking. Not a difficult job. When he'd been with the Pinkerton Agency, his assignments were always complicated and often included travel across the country.

He made his way down the bustling street. Late afternoon and the townsfolk were finishing their daily business.

As he walked, Dutch considered the situation with their mysterious prisoner. Something about Jonesy's surly attitude didn't sit right with him. They'd dealt with their share of troublesome characters passing through, but this felt different somehow. More sinister.

Shaking off the uneasy feeling, he arrived at a small home not far from the house he rented from Noah. He rapped his knuckles against the doorframe.

"Afternoon, Mrs. Heaton," Dutch called out as the door opened.

"Oh, Deputy McFarlin, good afternoon," Dorinda replied, a touch flustered. She smoothed her apron and ushered him inside. "To what do I owe the pleasure?"

Dutch removed his hat. "I'm just making my rounds. I wanted to extend an invitation to you and Joel to join me for supper at the boardinghouse this evening, if you're amenable."

"That's very kind of you. I'm sure Joel would love a break from his school lessons."

Dutch nodded. "Good. I'll come by at five o'clock to escort the two of you."

He turned to leave, then paused. "Say, how are things going at the school? I heard you have a full house of students these days."

Dorinda sighed. "Yes, I'm afraid we're fit to burst.

With the new families in town, more students keep arriving. We desperately need another teacher."

"I see." Dutch stroked his chin. "Well, let's discuss it more at supper."

Dorinda smiled, the worry in her eyes lessening a bit. "That would be wonderful. We'll be ready at five."

Dutch tipped his hat again and stepped back out into the waning sunlight, his mind churning over how to solve this new dilemma.

Dutch sat with Dorinda and her son, Joel, at a table in the boardinghouse. The aroma of roast beef filled the air, causing his stomach to rumble.

Joel picked at his food, uncharacteristically quiet. Dorinda glanced at her son with concern. "What's troubling you, Joel?"

The boy hesitated, then looked at Dutch. "I miss living at the ranch. All my friends are still there." Joel looked at his mother. "My father...do you think he'll ever come visit?"

An awkward silence descended on the table. Dorinda straightened in her seat, distress flitting across her face.

Dutch leaned forward, speaking gently. "Your father is a busy man, running his farm near Salt Lake. I'm sure he thinks of you often."

Joel's face fell. Dorinda reached out and squeezed

his hand.

Clearing his throat, Dutch changed tactics. "Say, how would you like to help me and Deputy Wheeler from time to time? We could use a sharp set of eyes like yours around town."

The boy perked up at that. "Really? You'd let me help?"

Dutch chuckled. "Sure, deputy in training. We'll make a lawman of you."

Joel grinned, his melancholy forgotten. Dorinda shot Dutch a grateful look.

"Now," Dutch said, "about this school situation..."

Morgan rode up to the orphanage, Jonesy's horse ponied behind him. Dismounting, he nodded in gratitude when one of the older boys offered to untack and feed them.

"Take good care of them." Morgan ruffled the boy's hair before turning toward the house.

He strode up the front steps. His thoughts were troubled, preoccupied with the outlaw locked up in the jail. He hoped Jonesy would talk soon, for the sake of the town's safety.

Inside, he found Martha in the main hall, surrounded by a pack of babbling children. She looked up with a smile as Morgan entered.

"Hello, Deputy."

Morgan tipped his hat. "How is everything going here?"

"Fine. The children are doing well." Martha's smile faded slightly. "The older ones are a little disappointed about not having the training today."

"We'll have the second class tomorrow."

"I'll let them know. Is the man you found outside in jail?"

Morgan hesitated. He didn't want to alarm her. "He's in jail. Still not talking. Be sure to let me or Tucker know if you see any strangers lurking about. It's the same for everyone here."

Martha nodded, her expression serious. "We will. Thank you, Morgan, for all you do to keep us safe. Cole will be back this evening. He wanted me to tell you he'll be taking a shift with you and Tucker."

Morgan touched the brim of his hat. "I'm going to find Tucker."

"He's out back with the children."

Morgan strode down the orphanage's back steps, spotting Tucker talking with a few of the older children. His friend hadn't noticed him. He hesitated, not wanting to interrupt the conversation.

He'd learned how hard it could be to get any of the orphans to talk and open up about their past or their future. The last was the most difficult. As the orphans approached the age when they were ex-pected to move on, he'd noticed their moods shift.

Many had few skills, no place to live, and no money for food. Fear gripped them as the date they were free to leave grew closer.

So far, those who'd left found jobs in Splendor. Noah had built two modest bunkhouses, one for women, the other for men, for any of the orphans who wanted a place to live. He supplied them with bedding, and charged little, as long as they kept the inside clean.

The small kitchen included a wood stove, pots, baking pans, dishes, and utensils. Once a month, Noah delivered flour, salt, sugar, and coffee to each bunkhouse. All these expenses were possible due to donations from businesses and neighboring ranchers.

Watching Tucker and the children, Morgan wondered what would happen to them when the town could no longer support their living expenses or offer them jobs.

Chapter Twelve

Cole stood on the top step of the orphanage's back porch, a satisfied smile crossing his rugged features. Morgan and Tucker stood nearby, their gazes moving over the yard and trees beyond.

Cole lowered his voice. "Gentlemen, I have an idea. What do you say we treat the ladies to a fine supper at the Eagle's Nest Saturday evening?"

Morgan's eyes lit up at the suggestion. "A great idea. They've been working themselves ragged at the orphanage. A night off is just what they need."

Tucker nodded enthusiastically. "I'm in, too. It'll be good for them to get out and enjoy themselves."

The men began discussing plans, their voices blending in animated chatter. Morgan suggested arriving at the orphanage by buggy to drive the women into town. Tucker offered to ask May Covington to bake one of her famous apple pies for dessert.

Soon, the conversation turned to who would watch the children during the excursion. Cole's brow furrowed. "That's the one hitch. We can't leave the children unattended."

Morgan leaned forward, rubbing his chin thoughtfully. "Why don't I ride out and ask Dutch if he'll keep an eye on things? The children have met him, and he's good with them. I'm sure he won't mind lending a hand."

Cole nodded. "Good idea."

The men shared a look of anticipation, already envisioning the women's delighted surprise at their thoughtfulness. Supper at the Eagle's Nest would be an evening to remember.

Cole straightened, a determined glint in his eye. "I'll stop at the restaurant tomorrow morning and make arrangements with Michael. Then I'll talk to Noah about a buggy."

The other men voiced their approval as Cole grabbed his shotgun and strode down the steps to walk the property. Morgan and Tucker followed him, each going in a different direction.

The following morning, Cole stepped inside the St. James, spotting Michael behind the front counter. The manager looked up and smiled in welcome. "Good morning, Deputy. What brings you by?"

He explained his plans for the ladies' supper Saturday night. Michael smiled. "A fine idea. I'll set aside the best table for you, right by the windows overlooking Frontier Street."

Michael glanced down at the guest ledger, running his finger over the pages. "I'll take care of it right now." Writing in the ledger, he set down his pen. "Five o'clock tomorrow. I'll even have a bottle of our best wine waiting. This will be an evening the ladies will never forget."

Cole grinned, visions of the women's delighted faces making his heart swell. "Much obliged, Michael."

With arrangements confirmed, Cole turned toward the door. Riding to the jail, he dismounted and tossed the reins over the post.

Cole strode toward the livery, thoughts filled with anticipation for the ladies' special supper. Heading along the boardwalk, he spotted Noah exiting the telegraph office.

"Good morning, Noah."

"Cole. Good to see you. What has you grinning like last year's fool?"

Cole chuckled. "I just reserved the best table at the Eagle's Nest for tomorrow evening. We're planning a surprise supper for Martha, Amelia, and Rose."

He outlined their plans.

Noah's mouth tipped into a grin. "Those ladies deserve something special after all their hard work at the orphanage. What do you need from me?"

"A buggy, if you can spare one. We want to take the women to the restaurant in style."

"I've got just the thing." He led Cole around back,

where a shiny black buggy stood waiting. Coming to an abrupt stop, Cole stared at the beautiful carriage, taking in the smooth lines and lacquered wood.

"I'll hitch up my two handsome buckskin geldings, and have her ready by four tomorrow afternoon. Those ladies will feel like royalty riding in this beauty."

Cole shook his friend's hand. "Much obliged, Noah. I'll bring her back first thing on Sunday morning."

With transportation secured, Cole began his rounds in town. He looked forward to sharing the news with Tucker and Morgan, hoping their enthusiasm matched his own. Tomorrow couldn't come soon enough.

Late the next afternoon, Cole pulled the gleaming black buggy up to the orphanage, spotting Tucker and Morgan on the porch. The three men, already cleaned up and wearing their best clothes, exchanged excited grins as they went to fetch the ladies.

"We have a surprise for you," Cole announced to Martha, barely containing his enthusiasm.

Martha, Amelia, and Rose looked at each other.

"What is it?" Amelia asked.

"It wouldn't be much of a surprise if we told you," Morgan answered. "Go get yourselves ready, we're taking you out for the evening."

The women hesitated, worried about leaving the children. Then the sound of a wagon pulling up had the three rushing to the front window. Dutch, Dorinda, and Joel walked up the steps and into the house.

"You ladies go and enjoy yourselves," Dutch said. "We'll take good care of the children."

Reassured, the women hurried off to change. Soon, they emerged in their Sunday best, fresh-faced and glowing. Cole helped them into the buggy, telling each one how lovely they looked.

The ride to town was filled with laughter and lighthearted chatter. When they arrived at the Eagle's Nest, Michael greeted them at the door. "Welcome! Your table is ready."

He led them to a table by the window, beautifully decorated with flowers and candles. The women gasped in delight as the men held their chairs.

"This is so wonderful!" Rose exclaimed, taking in the ambiance. "How did you ever plan all this?"

"We wanted to show our appreciation for three very special ladies," Cole said with a wink, picking up his menu.

Soon, they were all engrossed in eating the mouthwatering dishes and trading stories. The conversation ebbed and flowed, punctuated by moments of easy silence as they enjoyed the food and company.

As the evening progressed, they learned a lot about each other, and their reasons for coming to Splendor. Laughter rang out often, putting smiles on the faces of the other diners. For a few hours, chores and responsibilities faded away, leaving space for joy.

The group was finishing up the main course when Michael appeared with a large covered dish.

"We have saved the best for last," he announced, setting it down with a flourish. "With compliments from May."

He lifted the lid to reveal an apple pie, golden brown and oozing with juice. The spicy scent of cinnamon filled the air, making everyone's mouth water.

"Oh, my, it looks divine," Martha exclaimed.

Michael cut the pie and served it while May hovered nearby, eager to see their reactions. As soon as Amelia took a bite, her eyes widened.

"May, this is incredible." She slid her fork under another bite. "The flakiest crust I've ever had, and the apples are so tender. You've outdone yourself."

The others murmured in agreement as they savored each forkful. The cinnamon and sugar blended perfectly with the tart apples and flaky crust.

"This is surely the best apple pie in the whole territory," Tucker declared. "We're honored you made this just for us."

May beamed with pride. "It was my pleasure. I'm so glad you're enjoying it."

As the last crumbs were scooped from the plates, the group sat back with contented sighs.

Cole patted his stomach. "I don't think I could eat another bite. This was a mighty fine meal."

The others nodded. For a few moments, they enjoyed the lingering tastes and the satisfaction of full stomachs and good company.

After a while, Morgan stretched and stood. "I suppose we should head back, and relieve Dutch."

The women gathered their belongings while Cole left to fetch the buggy. The others expressed their thanks to Michael and May. Soon, they headed into the night, recalling favorite moments from the evening and looking forward to the next time.

Cole guided the buggy through the darkened streets, the clip-clop of hooves and rumble of wheels punctuating the peaceful night. Muted laughter and conversation flowed from the passengers as they reveled in the lingering joy of their evening together.

Leaving town, the buggy moved along the bumpy trail. Suddenly, the right front wheel hit a rut, followed by a heart-stopping crack. The wheel collapsed with a sharp snap, tilting the buggy.

"Whoa!" Cole yanked the reins, bringing the spooked horses to a halt. The women cried out in alarm as Morgan and Tucker jumped out to steady the buggy.

"Is everyone all right?" Morgan's face creased with concern.

A chorus of shaky confirmations answered him. Tucker knelt to examine the damaged wheel. "Broke an axle. We'll never make it back on this."

Cole secured the horses, joining Tucker on the ground. "We have less than a mile to the orphanage. I believe we can fix it good enough to get there."

The men set to work, their capable hands making

quick work of removing the wheel. As they conferred on the best way to repair it, Martha shivered and pulled her shawl tighter.

"It sure got cold quick," she murmured, unease nagging at her.

"Won't be long now," Cole assured her with a smile. Studying the damage, his eyes held a glint of worry belying his confident tone.

The group stiffened as hoofbeats thundered toward them, seeming to come from all directions at once. Startled cries rang out when eight hard-faced men on horseback materialized from the darkness, hemming them in. Rifles and pistols glinted in the moonlight as the riders trained their weapons on the stranded group.

Amelia gasped, gripping Rose's arm. The men froze, hands hovering over their holstered guns. A silent exchange passed between them as the severity of their situation sunk in.

Chapter Thirteen

Cole raised both hands, his eyes locked on the riders. "Evening, gentlemen. Something we can help you with?" His voice was steady, but his muscles tensed, ready to react.

A slender, sharp-boned man, with a grizzled beard, sneered down at them. "Yeah, you can hand over them horses." He pointed his rifle toward the women.

Morgan and Tucker exchanged a subtle glance. Tucker's hand drifted casually toward his hip.

"No need for trouble here," Cole said. "We'll be on our way as soon as we fix this wheel."

"Your way is back the way you came," the sharp-boned man growled. "Ain't nothing for you up ahead 'cept an early grave."

Morgan's eyes narrowed as he forced himself to relax.

Martha touched his arm. "Please, let's do as they say." Her wide eyes implored him to back down.

Jaw clenched, Morgan looked from her to the

riders and back again. He gave a curt nod.

Tucker hesitated, then withdrew his hand from his holster. The riders kept their weapons ready and watchful eyes on the group as Cole and Tucker removed the horses' harnesses.

"Appreciate your cooperation," the leader said with a mocking tip of his hat. "Now clear on outta here, unless you want trouble you ain't prepared for."

With that, the riders wheeled their mounts around and thundered off, driving the stolen horses ahead of them. The dust settled slowly in their wake as Cole laid a reassuring hand on Martha's back.

"It's all right now. Let's start walking."

The group exchanged shaken looks, then began the walk to the orphanage, their evening ruined but their lives intact.

Morgan let out a frustrated breath as they trekked to the home. He couldn't believe they'd given in so easily to those cowards. If it had been him and the other men, they could've put up a fight. But with the women, it was too risky.

Amelia walked beside Morgan, her earlier joy replaced by a somber expression. She glanced over at him. "I'm sorry. I know you wanted to stand up to them."

He gave her a gentle smile. "Wasn't worth risking anyone getting hurt over. I'm just glad you're safe."

Amelia nodded, a faint blush touching her cheeks. They continued in thoughtful silence.

Up ahead, Cole had his arm around Martha as they spoke in hushed tones. Trailing behind, Tucker kicked at stones along the road, his hat pulled low over his eyes.

Rose had drifted back from the others, her face turned up to the darkening sky. She fell into step beside Tucker. He looked over at her.

"You all right, Rose?"

She sighed. "I'm fine. Still, I wish there'd been something we could have done to defend ourselves. If I'd had a shotgun…"

"You would've blown them away."

"Absolutely." She shot him a grin, which Tucker returned with a chuckle.

Up ahead, Cole had tucked Martha's arm through his, whispering something that made her laugh. The sound carried on the night air, warm and welcome after the tension of their encounter.

Tucker's mood seemed to have improved as well. He was recounting some story to Rose, gesturing with his hands. She listened with a genuine smile, her eyes losing the shadow of unease Tucker had seen earlier.

Morgan kept his eyes focused on the dark road ahead as the others chatted around him and Amelia. Glancing at her, he moved closer, settling his arm over her shoulders.

As they walked, he was still rattled by the confrontation with the mysterious riders. Who were they? And how had they known where to find them on this remote stretch of road?

Unease gnawed at him. Something wasn't right. He strained his ears for any sound of approaching hooves, hearing only the steady thumping of boots on the hard ground.

Up ahead, the oil lamps inside the orphanage came into view, glowing in welcome. Almost home. Morgan felt himself relax.

Cole and Tucker rode into town the following morning, heading straight to the livery. Noah stood with his hands on his hips, staring at the small apartment above the storeroom.

Cole's face was etched with grim determination while Tucker chewed his lower lip. Neither looked forward to the conversation with Noah.

"Morning, Cole. Tucker." He glanced behind the two deputies. They knew why.

"We have bad news," Cole said.

Noah walked toward them. "What is it?"

"Well, the buggy broke down on the way home last night. We think it's the axle. The bigger problem is, when we tried to fix it, eight bandits surrounded us."

"They took my horses."

"We're dang sorry, Noah," Tucker said.

"I'll pay you for them," Cole added. "It's my fault for the breakdown. I drove the buggy over a real deep rut in the trail. I'm sure that's what caused the axle to break."

"Cole, the entire trail from town to the orphanage

is one long rut. And I'm guessing the bandits said they'd shoot you if you didn't give them the horses. Nothing else you could've done, not with the three women as easy targets."

"I'm sure the gang would've shot them," Cole said. "Tell me what I owe for the horses, and I'll get the money to you."

"No need."

"Don't try talking me out of it, Noah. Also, we'll need to get the buggy fixed and back to you. It's not far from the orphanage."

"Did the wheel break?"

"It cracked," Cole said.

"I can take a wagon out, fix the axle, and replace the broken wheel. I'll need someone to drive the wagon back to town."

"I'll do that, Noah."

"Thanks, Tucker. Check with Gabe and let me know when you can head out there with me."

"Will do."

Riding to the jail and dismounting, they entered to find Gabe pouring himself a cup of coffee. He took a quick look at his deputies, seeing their drawn expressions.

"Morning, boys." Sitting down, he motioned for them to do the same. "By your faces, it appears you have something to tell me."

Cole nodded and explained what had happened. "There were eight of them, Gabe. They took the horses and nothing else. Didn't hurt anyone."

"They just rode off," Tucker said.

Cole nodded. "Their leader was a tall, wiry fellow with stringy gray hair. A nasty looking son-of-a-gun."

Gabe's expression darkened. He opened a drawer and pulled out a wanted poster, sliding it across the desk. "Did he look like him?"

Cole and Tucker studied the sketch on the poster. The sharp angles of the face, piercing eyes, and hair left no doubt about the man's identity. Dean Shaw.

"That's him all right," Tucker confirmed. "Says here he's the head of the Wyoming Highwaymen. Catchy name."

Gabe muttered something under his breath. He stood abruptly, his chair scraping against the wooden floor. "Dean Shaw started out in Nebraska, made his way to Missouri, then decided Texas was a target too big to pass up. I heard he'd gone to Wyoming. If he's in these parts, the whole town could be in danger. We need to spread the word and get folks prepared."

He walked to the front window to look out. "If his routine holds true, Shaw is known for hitting an area and leaving. The man doesn't stick around."

"You're saying he may have stolen the horses and left?" Cole asked.

"It's a definite possibility. Since we don't know, we must spread the word without causing panic." Gabe narrowed his gaze on Cole. "After the outlaws who tried to kidnap Camilla the previous summer, this is the last thing Splendor needs."

He began issuing orders, his calm demeanor replaced by firm resolve. Cole and Tucker listened, ready to do whatever it took to keep their town safe.

"One more thing," Gabe added. Both deputies paused. "One of you stop by the telegraph office and send word to my brother, U.S. Marshal Chan Evans. He's in Big Pine, ready to transport a man to Deer Lodge prison. The government will want to know Dean Shaw was spotted in Splendor. Also, send telegrams to Sheriff Parker Sterling and the sheriff in Laramie."

"Yes, sir," Cole assured him. With a glance at Tucker, they headed out.

While Cole walked down the boardwalk to the telegraph office, Tucker began spreading the word. Both knew there was a good chance Shaw and his gang had left after stealing the horses. Or they could break from past actions and be holed up somewhere near the town, with plans to hit another target. If they didn't ride on, there was no time to waste.

Gabe watched them go, jaw tight. If Shaw was coming to Splendor's doorstep, he aimed to be ready. He sighed, settling back into his desk chair. It was going to be a long few days.

Cole and Tucker met up an hour later at the Dixie saloon, deciding to head back to the jail. As they strode along the boardwalk, shopkeepers paused their sweeping to stare while other townsfolk darted wary glances their way.

Reaching the jail, Cole shoved the door open, finding the sheriff at his desk. Gabe's jaw was set, his brows drawn together.

"Tucker, ride out and alert the MacLarens," he ordered. "Cole, notify the Pelletiers. Ask them to be on alert for Shaw and his gang."

The afternoon sun touched the top of the mountains to the west as Tucker and Cole helped Noah fix the buggy. Each glanced up from their work often to scan the area.

Even with three men, the repairs took longer than Noah had hoped. When finished, Cole sent Tucker on to the orphanage while he drove the wagon back to the livery.

Jumping to the ground, Cole removed the harness and lines from the horse, leading it back to its stall. When Noah stopped the buggy behind the livery, Cole helped him with the horse before reaching into a pocket. Pulling out a bank draft, he handed it to Noah.

"What's this?"

"A start on what I owe for the horses."

Noah shook his head. "It's a start and end, Cole. This will cover their cost and help me locate another pair." He held out his hand. "Thank you."

"I'm just sorry they're gone." Retrieving his horse

from its stall, he swung into the saddle. "I'd better get to the orphanage."

"Be safe out there, Cole. If you need more men, let me know."

Chapter Fourteen

It had been a week since anyone had seen or heard from Dean Shaw and his band of outlaws, the Wyoming Highwaymen. An uneasy quiet had settled over the town, bringing hope the gang may not return.

Morgan Wheeler sat on the bench outside the sheriff's office, seeking refuge in the narrow strip of shade it provided while whittling a piece of wood. He glanced up the street, hoping to catch a glimpse of Amelia. They'd arrived in town early so she could complete her errands before noon.

Hearing the distinct sound of boots on the boardwalk, he glanced in the opposite direction. Gabe strode toward him.

"Got word from a sheriff in Utah," Gabe said without preamble. "The Highwaymen hit a group of settlers a few miles from Salt Lake City the day before last."

Morgan straightened. "They've moved on then?"

"Seems so. At least for now." He looked across the

street at a couple of men stumbling out of the Dixie. "We shouldn't get complacent, though. Never know when those snakes might slither back into our valley."

Morgan followed the sheriff's gaze, grinning at the antics of the two cowboys. Still morning and those two were beyond drunk.

He thought of what Gabe had said. The Wyoming Highwaymen may have fled for now, but they'd left uncertainty and apprehension lingering behind. Splendor was peaceful right now.

Could it be a false calm, lulling the town into mistaken harmony? Danger still lurked somewhere out there, requiring the town to remain vigilant.

"Best we keep our eyes peeled and our rifles loaded." Gabe's words pulled Morgan from his thoughts. "Trouble has a way of turning back up when you least expect it."

Morgan nodded, knowing the sheriff was right. They had to stay alert.

"I want Tucker back in town, in case those snakes circle back." Gabe shot a look in the opposite direction. "Dutch went through the wanted posters. He found one where the image matched Jonesy. His real name is Tate Smith." Gabe pulled it from a pocket, showing it to Morgan. "Says he rode with the Wyoming Highwaymen. Cash and Beau are taking him to Big Pine, where Sheriff Sterling will talk to the judge about a trial. They left early this morning."

Morgan understood the implications. With two of the most experienced deputies gone, and him stationed at the orphanage, the town was vulnerable if the outlaws returned. They'd have to be extra vigilant.

"I'll send Tucker back when Amelia and I return to the orphanage," he said.

Gabe gave a terse nod and headed off. Morgan watched him go, then turned back to gazing down the street leading out of town. Somewhere out there, the Highwaymen could be biding their time, waiting to strike near Splendor again.

Or the gang might be halfway to California, where they could ply their trade and disappear inside the thousands of people who'd settled there in the last thirty years.

Morgan slid his knife and piece of wood into a pocket before searching for Amelia. He'd promised her lunch at the boardinghouse after her morning errands. Things had been going well between them, a new closeness forming, giving Morgan a spark of hope for the future. He cherished their long conversations after the children were put to bed, the leisurely walks they took around the orphanage, and the brush of her hand against his, making his heart race.

Morgan had begun to believe he could have both—a life as a lawman and a family of his own. With Amelia by his side, both seemed possible.

Morgan found Amelia chatting with Olivia McCord outside the Splendor Emporium. She flashed him a smile, causing his heart to flutter.

"Good morning, ladies." Morgan tipped his hat. "I hope I'm not interrupting."

"Not at all," Olivia said. She and Josie Lucero

owned what townsfolk dubbed the finest general store in Montana. "Amelia and I were discussing the orphanage's need for more supplies before winter sets in. She's going to get me a list so I can pass it around town. Well, I'd better get back inside. So good to see you two."

He turned to Amelia, appreciating the sight of her auburn curls peeking out from under her bonnet.

"Shall we?"

She looped her arm through his, and they headed down the street toward the wagon. At first, they walked in comfortable silence, enjoying each other's company. Even with her beside him, Morgan's mind was troubled.

"Believing the Highwaymen are gone doesn't sit right with me," he admitted. "I'm afraid we may not have seen the last of Dean Shaw."

"I agree. I can't help worrying they'll return." She paused. "There are times I wish you weren't a deputy."

Morgan stiffened. "It's my job, Amelia. I was hired to help protect Splendor from threats such as Shaw."

"I know. When you care about someone, you don't want to see them get hurt. Or worse..."

Morgan stopped, turning to face her. "I'm not planning on getting hurt. I became a lawman to help folks, and that's what I'm going to do."

Amelia bit her lip. Morgan could see her struggling with her feelings.

"You don't have to be a lawman to protect the town. Look at Noah, Nick Barnett, or any number of people. They have regular jobs, yet when there's trouble, they stand beside the sheriff and his deputies."

His voice took on a frustrated tone. "What would you have me do, Amelia? I have no skills except what I learned on the family farm. There's no money to buy land of my own. And there are my siblings to consider. As a deputy, I'm able to send money home." He turned away from her, taking several steps along the boardwalk.

"I'm sorry, Morgan. It isn't fair of me to put this burden on you." Closing the distance between them, he didn't accept her outstretched hand.

"Why don't you apply for the teaching job in town?" he prodded gently. "Give yourself something more to do than fret about me."

Amelia's eyes flashed. "I don't need you telling me what to do." She crossed the street, walking briskly toward the wagon.

Morgan hurried after her. "Now, hold on, I didn't mean..."

His words were lost as shouts rang out down the street. People were pointing west, toward the mountains. Morgan and Amelia froze, following their gazes. A line of smoke was rising in the distance.

"Fire," Morgan muttered. He grabbed Amelia's hand. "Come on!"

They raced to the wagon, hearts pounding with the threat looming before them.

People were gathering in the street, their faces etched with concern as they stared at the rising plume of smoke. This was the kind of threat the residents dreaded.

Frontier towns faced many dangers, the most frightening was fire. A hot burn with moderate wind could destroy wood buildings in minutes. Adding the dry summer with little rain, Morgan knew Splendor was a powder keg, ready to explode.

"Where's it coming from?" Amelia asked, joining the crowd.

"West of here, up in the high country." Bernie Griggs pointed while bouncing on the balls of his feet.

Morgan scanned the mountains. The smoke grew thicker by the minute, billowing up in a massive column, darkening the sky.

"With this drought, a fire could reach town in a very short period of time." Morgan's worried gaze bored into Amelia. "You should get back to the orphanage, let Martha know what's coming."

Panic flashed in her eyes. "Do you think we'll have to evacuate the house?"

He squeezed her hand. "I'm not sure yet. To be safe, get the children out of there and up the hill."

Gabe joined the crowd, his face streaked with worry. "Fire's moving fast," he reported. "I've already talked with the other deputies. We have to get everyone ready to clear out if it jumps the ridge."

Morgan nodded. Around them, people erupted into worried murmurs.

Gabe raised his voice. "I want every able-bodied person helping however they can. Check on your neighbors and assist anyone who needs help getting away from the path of the fire. And stay calm."

His eyes met Morgan's, conveying the seriousness of the situation. Morgan steeled himself, turning toward Amelia, seeing the anxiety in her eyes. Leaning down, he spoke against her ear.

"You did great during the flood last summer. You'll do as well with the fire." Straightening, he stared at the crowd.

"You heard the sheriff. Let's move."

Amelia nodded, her lips pressed into a determined line. She looked at Morgan, admiring the way he took control when Gabe moved down the street. His job was here, helping the people. Her place was at the orphanage.

Pushing aside their earlier disagreements in the face of this new threat, she climbed onto the wagon, grabbing the reins. Slapping the lines, her heart pounded with purpose.

Glancing over her shoulder, she slapped the lines again. Smoke billowed ever closer, threatening all she held dear.

Morgan hurried through the chaotic streets, shouting for people to pack essential items and evacuate. While ushering residents to the edge of town, he never let his attention move far from the fire's location.

"Stay together!" Morgan called out as families clutched children and possessions. "Head for the creek just east of Old Ida's cabin. We'll regroup there."

He grasped the arm of an elderly woman struggling with a large trunk. "Here, let me help you with that."

The woman relinquished her grip, face pale. "Bless you, dear. These old bones aren't what they used to be."

Morgan hefted the trunk, muscles straining. Glancing back, he saw Jonas lifting a young boy onto his horse before turning to help a man with a limping gait.

Glancing west, his throat tightened as flames licked the treetops several miles away. To some, it would seem they still had a lot of time to evacuate. Morgan knew better. Fires moved faster than most understood. He had to get the people to move faster.

Gunshots rang out nearby, followed by shouts. Morgan's head jerked up, hand flying to his holster. A group of men poured from a side street, grappling with each other.

One raised a smoking pistol skyward, firing. "I ain't leaving my shop to burn!" Herb Caulfield, owner of the meat market, bellowed.

Morgan strode over, grabbing his wrist to release the gun from the older man's hand. "Mr. Caulfield, you'll do as the sheriff ordered," he growled. "Your shop can be rebuilt. Your life can't."

Caulfield scowled but let his arm drop. Morgan

motioned for two other men to take him to the evacuation point.

Morgan wiped sweat from his brow, streaking dirt across his forehead. The hot, dry winds carried the acrid smell of smoke and the distant roar of the flames. He'd been working for hours to evacuate the town, knowing there were still stragglers reluctant to abandon their homes and businesses.

Ruby Walsh, owner of the Grand Palace, emerged from between two buildings, supporting an elderly man with a hacking cough. Morgan hurried over to take the man's other arm.

"That's the last one on this street," Ruby said, voice raspy from the smoke.

They moved through the haze as quickly as the old man could manage. All around, buildings stood empty, doors flung open, possessions abandoned. What had been a thriving town had become a ghost town in a short few hours.

Smoke and ash created a dirty haze over Splendor, making it hard for many to breathe. The older residents were the most at risk.

At last, they reached the edge of town, where wagons were gathered, filled with those unable to ride or walk. A makeshift medical station had been assembled. Doctors McCord and Rawlins, plus two nurses, and a few volunteers, treated injuries and smoke inhalation.

Morgan and Ruby helped the old man onto a wagon bench. She squeezed his hand. "You'll be all right now."

The man nodded weakly, eyes brimming with tears. "My home..."

"They're just things." Ruby patted his knee. "We can rebuild."

As she turned away, Morgan saw her swipe discreetly at her own eyes. He knew she was thinking of the Grand Palace, wondering if the building would live through the fire or be reduced to ashes.

Morgan thought of Amelia and the orphanage, wondering if the women and children were safe.

Chapter Fifteen

Amelia, Rose, and Martha hurriedly loaded armfuls of supplies into the back of the wagon. Sacks of food, bundles of blankets, baskets of fruit, and extra clothes were loaded with care. The three women worked in tense silence, sweat beading on their foreheads as the distant roar of the approaching fire filled the air.

"That's the last of the food," Amelia said, her voice tight as she secured the final sack. Her thoughts raced as she took stock of what they'd managed to gather. Was it enough? Would the children have food to eat if they were forced to flee farther than expected?

Rose scrambled out of the wagon, dusting off her skirt. "I'll do one more sweep to make sure we didn't miss anything important." She tried to sound confident, but her hands trembled as she turned back toward the house.

Martha caught Rose's arm, giving it a gentle, steadying squeeze. "Only the most critical items. We need to leave right away." Though her wealthy upbringing in Boston hadn't prepared her for this, she was determined to hold the makeshift family together.

Rose nodded, blinking back tears. She rushed into the house while Martha and Amelia hurried to gather the children.

Amidst the chaos, Martha's voice rang out, clear and steady. "Children, come here, please!" She beckoned them closer as Amelia herded them into a small cluster. "I know you're scared, but we need to stay together now."

The children huddled in a tight group, holding onto each other, wide-eyed. Amelia put a comforting arm around two of the youngest girls. "Shhh, it's all right."

Martha scanned the group, putting on a brave face. "Older children, I need your help. Can you partner up with the younger ones and make sure they stay with us?"

The older kids nodded, taking the hands of their smaller charges.

Rose emerged with an armful of extra coats. "These were in the basement," she said, her voice wavering. Martha smiled at her, a wordless message of courage passing between them.

"Please walk in a group ahead of the wagon." Martha took up the reins, steadying her nerves. She clucked her tongue, spurring the horses forward as they began what she hoped was a short journey.

Martha guided the wagon up the hill, the horses

straining with effort. The children trudged ahead of her, wide eyes peering behind them at the advancing flames.

Amelia thought of something, grabbed two of the older boys, Jacob and Marcus, and ran back toward the house. They disappeared inside, emerging moments later. Amelia carried two rifles and a large sack of ammunition while the boys each held shotguns and revolvers.

Martha looked back at them as they reached the wagon. "Hurry now! We must keep moving."

Amelia and the boys placed their haul into the wagon, except for one shotgun, which she kept. She took a position beside the wagon, gun at the ready.

At the top of the hill, they turned to look at the fire's progress. Though still a good distance away, it raged through the valley below, consuming trees and brush. The orphanage and town were still safe, for now. Everyone knew it was only a matter of time before they were consumed by flames.

Martha felt tears prick her eyes. Establishing the orphanage had taken a huge effort, both in money and manpower. Now, they could only watch, helpless to stop the approaching flames.

Martha turned to the children. "All right, everyone. We're going to keep moving. I know you're tired, but we need to move farther away." Her encouragement bolstered the children's flagging spirits.

Amelia kept her shotgun ready, scanning the surrounding woods for any sign of danger. She knew fire drove all manner of creatures from their dens.

Desperate animals could pose as much a threat as the flames themselves.

Her thoughts turned to Morgan, wondering where he was, and prayed he was safe.

Gabe stopped his evacuation efforts to bend over, coughing from the smoke and ash in the air. Straightening, he turned to the deputies waiting for orders.

"Let's make one last sweep of town," he shouted. "We're moving everyone to the creek east of Old Ida's cabin." The deputies dispersed, walking the town street by street, clearing buildings.

Despite the chaos and his fear for the orphanage, Morgan focused on his job. Checking each building and house on his route, he didn't find any stragglers. He spotted Gabe in front of the St. James.

"Sheriff, we need to check on the orphanage, see if they need help. I want to ride out, make sure they get clear of the fire."

Gabe frowned, clearly torn. People in town still needed help. He also knew the children at the orphanage were just as vulnerable.

"All right," Gabe conceded. "Go on and do what you can. Take Cole with you. We'll manage things here." He shook both men's hands. "Good luck, and be careful."

Morgan and Cole mounted up and spurred their

horses toward the orphanage. The sky glowed an ominous orange as smoke blotted out the sun. Morgan's eyes burned.

When they reached the orphanage, Cole dismounted to run inside. Returning, he shook his head.

"They're gone." Cole mounted, reining his horse around.

Morgan rode to where he could see the hill to the east. He spotted the wagon.

"They're headed up the hill. The wagon is struggling to get up the rocky slope. We need to get to them."

Kicking their horses' flanks, they took off.

Martha coaxed the overburdened horses onward. Amelia and Rose shepherded the children, most doing well despite the danger.

Something had Amelia glancing over her shoulder, relief flooding her. "Morgan and Cole are here."

The men dismounted. Cole climbed onto the seat next to Martha, taking the lines. Morgan handed his reins to one of the older girls, he motioned for the older boys to join him.

"Let's push from the back, boys." They didn't hesitate.

Step by agonizing step, they fought their way to a higher spot on the hill.

At the summit, they stopped, most everyone fighting exhaustion.

Martha hugged Cole, relief washing over her. "Thank you..."

Amelia grasped Morgan's hand. "I'm so glad you

came," she whispered. He nodded, words failing him.

In the distance, they could see the fire had moved to within a quarter mile of town. It would take longer to reach the orphanage.

Morgan stared at the approaching flames, a mix of emotions swirling within him. Relief knowing the children were safe for now. Sorrow at what would happen when the fire reached the orphanage and town.

The children huddled nearby, their wide eyes staring into the distance.

Cole stood with his arm around Martha. He felt a change in the air.

"The wind seems to be shifting." He looked at Morgan. "If it keeps up, we may be spared."

Morgan felt the shift, too. Lifting his head, his breath caught.

"Look there." He pointed upward. Dark clouds were moving from the south to blanket the mountains.

"Rain clouds," Cole said.

All heads tilted upward, watching as a large mass of darkness moved their way. As if hesitant to hope, no one spoke.

The quiet continued for several minutes before one of the children shrieked, swiping at her face. "It's raining!"

The relief was intense, but Morgan knew the danger hadn't been eliminated. There were still smoldering embers ready to reignite if the rain clouds raced north.

Cole steered the wagon down the hill, attempting to avoid being caught in a mudslide. Behind him, Morgan escorted the ladies and children to the orphanage. Even as the rain continued to fall, everyone basked in a celebratory mood.

The men, and two of the older boys, unloaded the wagon while the women settled the children and unpacked the boxes. Exhaustion was evident on all faces.

Amelia put together a simple meal of cold chicken, biscuits, and jam. Filling their stomachs, Cole and Morgan excused themselves.

"I'd stay, but I should be in town, helping people move back into their homes." Morgan searched Amelia's eyes, finding understanding.

"I understand. It's a certainty a few of the children will have trouble sleeping. The fire scared many of them. We both have jobs to do."

A weary smile appeared. "Yes, we do." He wanted to kiss her. Grabbing her hand, he drew her to the front door, bending his head to capture her mouth. After a moment, he lifted his head. "I'll be back as soon as I can."

"You ready?" Cole walked past them on his way outside.

"Ready."

Martha and Amelia stood on the porch, watching

as the men disappeared down the road.

"I don't know if we would've made it up the hill without Cole and Morgan," Martha said. "I'm so thankful Gabe sent them to us."

"No matter what, we would've gotten the children up the hill. Not sure about the wagon. We may have overloaded it a bit." She smiled at Martha. "Thank goodness for the rain. We would've lost the orphanage and the town without it."

Amelia continued to watch the road, knowing the men were well on their way to town.

Chapter Sixteen

Morgan wiped the sweat from his brow as he stepped back to survey the progress. All around him, people were carrying personal belongings, wiping down windows, and sweeping up piles of ash. Though the wildfire had never reached Splendor itself, it had left a coat of grimy residue over everything.

"This town sure is resilient," Jonas said as he hauled a small crate into the general store.

Morgan nodded. "It is."

Tucker strode up holding two canvas bags overflowing with new clothes. "Guess these go in the general store, too."

"Hard to believe a little smoke and ash could cause so much damage," Jonas said.

Morgan sighed. "It was a miracle the town didn't burn down. Makes you appreciate the simple things. Having a roof over your head and a warm meal."

His thoughts drifted to Amelia, as they often did these days. He longed to see her, to set things right between them. But duty called, and the townspeople needed him.

"Well, don't go getting all sentimental on us now." Jonas chuckled. "Come on, we've got plenty more to haul."

The men headed back out into the street. All around them, the residents of Splendor worked side by side, smiles showing on weary faces. Hardship had only made them kinder, brought them closer together.

Spotting Bernie Griggs trying to clean the sign above the telegraph office, Morgan jogged over.

"Let me help you." Morgan cleaned the upper part of the sign while Bernie worked on the lower half. Together, they stepped back to admire their work.

Out of the corner of his eye, he caught sight of the mountain ridge in the distance, its usual vibrant green replaced by swaths of blackened trees and charred underbrush. The fire had carved a narrow path straight down the mountainside, leaving devastation in its wake.

Morgan stared at the contrast between the scorched earth and the untouched sections of the mountain range. It was strange, almost unnatural, the way the fire had burned.

"Hey, Morgan. You all right?" Jonas noticed his friend's furrowed brow.

"Hmm? Oh yeah, I'm fine. Just thinking is all."

Jonas followed his gaze up to the mountain. "Yeah, it's a mighty strange sight. Seems the fire would've spread wider than it did. I wonder what started the fire in the first place?"

"Don't know," Morgan replied. His thoughts had already drifted back to Amelia, despite his best efforts. He missed her fiercely.

If only he could find the right words to bridge the rift between them. He understood her hesitations about building a life with a lawman. Though not always, his job could be dangerous. It paid all right, allowing him to send money home to his siblings. He couldn't make the same kind of money doing anything else.

Jonas gave a light punch to Morgan's arm. "Let's get back to work."

Morgan pushed aside his questions about him and Amelia. The town needed him, and he aimed to see it through.

Cole rode up to the orphanage, his horse kicking up a cloud of ash and dust. Though exhaustion tugged at his limbs, his heart lifted at the sight of the familiar building.

He swung down from the saddle and handed the reins to one of the older boys who came running up.

"Evening, Deputy Santori. Mrs. Santori said to tell you we've got your supper waiting inside."

Cole smiled, removing his hat. "Thank you."

The boy nodded and led the horse away while Cole climbed the front steps. As soon as he entered, he looked up to see Martha descending the stairs, a tender smile on her face. She came forward and wrapped her arms around him.

"I'm so glad you're home." She pulled back to look at him. "How are you?"

"Tired. Hungry."

"I can help with both." Taking his hand in hers, she led him down the hall to the dining room. "Food first. Then bed."

Cole allowed her to lead him to the dining room. Martha's presence soothed his weary soul in a way nothing else could.

She sat beside him as he ate a large portion of stew and four biscuits. When finished, he sat back with a long sigh.

"That was excellent."

"Do you want more?"

"I've had plenty, sweetheart. Thank you for holding some back for me."

She laughed. "As if I wouldn't. How is the town looking?"

"Most everyone is moved back into their homes, and businesses are opening. Almost everything had to be scrubbed down from the ash. Considering what could've happened, cleaning up seems minor."

"You're right. We were much too close to losing the town and orphanage. I don't know what we would've done if we lost the house. Where would the children have gone?"

Covering her hand with his, he kissed her cheek. "Be thankful you don't have to worry about it any longer."

Morgan took a deep breath as he dismounted his horse outside the orphanage. It had been over a week since he'd last spoken to Amelia after the rains ended the threat of fire. Though his duties in town had kept him busy, she was never far from his thoughts.

He removed his hat and raked a hand through his dark hair before ascending the front steps. His heart pounded as he raised his hand to knock.

The door opened to reveal Amelia, surprise flickering across her delicate features. "Morgan. I wasn't expecting you."

"I know," he said softly. "May I come in?"

"Of course." She drew the door wide. "Have you eaten?"

"Before I rode out of town. With Tucker and Jonas at the boardinghouse."

"It's open already?"

"Suzanne reopened the day after the fire." Setting his hat on a hook, he looked at her. "Do you have a moment? I'd like to talk."

She studied him for a long moment before nodding. "Do we need quiet and privacy?"

"Both would be nice."

"Then we should sit on the front porch." Amelia turned toward the front door.

Morgan reached it first, pulling it open. She walked by him, taking a seat at one of several chairs.

He took a seat next to her.

"Until a few days ago, we couldn't sit outside. The remaining smoke made it hard to breathe. Was it the same in town?"

"It's still difficult to be outside for more than a few minutes. Unless you wear a handkerchief."

"You and the deputies?"

"Anyone working outside. The air here is much cleaner than in town."

She perched on the edge of the chair. "You wanted to talk?"

He nodded. "First, I want to apologize for the way I spoke to you last week. My words were callous. You deserved better."

Amelia looked down at her hands resting in her lap. "I accept your apology."

"I know you care deeply for the children here," Morgan continued. "I never meant to imply otherwise. It's one of the things I admire most about you."

"Admire?"

"Truly," Morgan insisted. "The love and compassion you show them is incredible. I worry you're taking on too much."

"What I do is no more than Rose or Martha. We all put in long hours. And we do it because we love the children."

He hesitated before forging ahead. "It's obvious how dedicated you are to the children. You rarely take a day off. I know from being here, you work twelve to fourteen hours every day. It leaves little time for anything else." He met her gaze. "Or anyone else."

Amelia's eyes widened on the last. Her lips parted on a breath before she looked away. The silence grew tense after neither spoke for several minutes. Morgan broke the silence.

"I care for you, Amelia. A great deal." He took several breaths before continuing. "My hope was we could build a life together, have children of our own. I still want a future with you. It's just, well...your priorities and mine are so far apart. I'm not certain it's possible."

Amelia's eyes glistened with unshed tears. "I care about you, too, Morgan. I'm sorry I pushed you away, made you believe a life without you was all right." She swallowed. "It's not all right."

Morgan reached for her hand, relief washing over him when she let him take it. "I understand this is your calling. I only want to support you, not take it from you."

"I know," Amelia whispered. "And I understand how much being a deputy means to you. It was selfish of me to ask you to find other work. I'm sorry."

Morgan brought her hand to his lips, kissing her knuckles. He held her hand gently, looking into her eyes with sincerity.

"I know there are still issues we need to work through," he said. "But I believe if we keep talking and listening to each other, we can find a way to compromise."

A tentative smile curled her lips. "I'd like that very much. I don't want our differences to tear us apart."

Morgan stroked his thumb over her knuckles.

"Neither do I. What we have is too important to just walk away from over a disagreement."

"Yes, it is."

Joy surged through Morgan. Standing, he drew her up into an embrace.

For a long moment, they held each other. Although there was still much to discuss, the hope they shared kindled a flame of optimism.

As Morgan held Amelia close, his mind drifted to the obstacles still remaining between them. Though they had reconciled for now, there were still difficult conversations to be had about their differing desires for the future.

Amelia longed to continue her life at the orphanage, while Morgan had found a home as a deputy. Could they find a compromise, a way to build a life together, with each pursuing their passions?

Morgan knew the shadows in his own heart and mind would linger. Doubts and worries weren't so easily banished.

Sighing, he knew the path ahead would not be easy. But he clung to hope, a flickering light to guide them through the unknown.

Tomorrow would bring new challenges. Tonight, they'd found their way back to each other.

Chapter Seventeen

The next morning, Morgan awoke before dawn, the responsibilities of the day already weighing on his mind. Careful not to disturb anyone, he slipped out from under the covers of the bed Amelia had made up for him in the library.

After getting dressed, he crept into the kitchen, removing two biscuits from a tin and spreading them with jam. By the time he stepped into the cool morning air, he'd eaten both.

The sun peeked over the mountains as he tacked up his horse and set off for town. Keeping his gaze moving over the trail, he thought about the discussion between him and Amelia. As promising as it had seemed, he knew there was a great deal more to work out before a decision about a shared future could be made.

Reaching the edge of town, the early stirrings of activity drew his attention. Shopkeepers swept the boardwalk, Bernie waved as he unlocked the telegraph office door, and Deputy Mack Mackey leaned against a post outside the jail.

All normal. So different from the day of the fire.

Reining up, he swung to the ground, tossing the reins over a post. Dutch strode out of the jail, holding a cup of coffee.

"How's everything at the orphanage?" Dutch asked.

"All's well and back to normal. The air out their way is better than what we have here."

"That so?" Dutch took a sip of coffee and smiled. "The coffee Gabe brings in from New York is the best around."

"Except for the St. James and boardinghouse," Mack said. "He takes our coffee out of their shipments."

Edging past Dutch, Morgan entered the jail to find it empty. Jonesy, their sole prisoner in weeks, had been escorted to Big Pine for trial. Noisy and obnoxious, he at least added a bit of life in the early morning hours.

He poured a cup of coffee, relishing the aroma before taking a sip. The premium brew would've gone well with his earlier breakfast of biscuits and jam. He'd wager few lawmen across the country could boast about their jailhouse coffee.

Lowering himself into one of the hard chairs, he thought again about his conversation with Amelia the night before. He'd avoided mentioning the teacher position, which had been approved before the fire. Dutch had been the one to bring the issue to Gabe's attention. He'd spoken to Stan and others responsible for the school. A few days later, the second teaching position had been authorized.

Morgan didn't see a reason for her not to interview for the job. Accepting an offer didn't eliminate volunteering at the orphanage, or cooking for them on weekends. He'd even go with her on his days off.

An idea flashed in his head. Was she disinterested in the teaching job because of concern over finding a cook to replace her? Knowing Amelia, it was a good guess.

Maybe the hesitancy was due to him pushing the opportunity on her. She was a proud, independent woman who insisted on making her own decisions.

Having many questions and no answers, he refilled his cup, almost emptying the pot. Grabbing the extra one, he prepared another pot. Setting it on the stove, he stoked the fire, returning to his chair.

Before sitting down, he heard shouts from outside. The voices grew louder, raised in some heated exchange. He set down his cup and strode to the door, senses on high alert.

Morgan stepped outside to see Mack and Dutch standing tense and rigid, engaged in conversation with three men he didn't recognize.

The men looked haggard, their clothes dusty from travel, their faces etched with desperation. They carried no weapons he could see. He noted the way Mack's hands were relaxed at his sides while Dutch stood with his arms crossed, expression stark.

As Morgan approached, the eldest of the three men broke off from arguing with Mack and turned to him, eyes pleading.

"Please, sir, you have to help us. We've been traveling for weeks with our families. The sheriff in Big Pine said he believed there might be jobs in Splendor. We're living in our wagons east of town." The man pointed behind him, before gesturing to the two younger men beside him.

"These are my sons. Both are married with young children. Our supplies are almost gone. We'll do any work, anything at all, in exchange for food."

Morgan studied the men. He knew the town had been struggling to accommodate all the newcomers pouring in, but turning away honest men in need sat ill with him.

Before he could respond, Mack shook his head. "Wish I knew of something, but I don't. The church keeps stores of food. You could check there, then you might consider moving on."

The man opened his mouth to object, but Morgan lifted a hand. "These folks have come a long way. The least we can do is sit down and talk it through. The supplies at the church are a good idea. Maybe we'll come up with other suggestions once we hear them out."

After a moment, Mack grunted acquiescence. With a gesture, Morgan invited the men into the jailhouse. Their shoulders sagged with relief and exhaustion.

As the men filed past him into the jailhouse, Morgan noticed Gabe approaching. He touched the brim of his hat in greeting as the sheriff reached them.

"Morning. Seems we've got a situation here with some newcomers."

Gabe's expression was somber as he studied the men. "Let's get inside, and we'll listen to what they have to say." His voice was gruff, but not unkind.

Morgan nodded. He respected Gabe and the way he handled difficult situations.

As they turned to go inside, Horace Clausen crossed the street, no doubt from hearing the commotion. The president of the town bank was known for his shrewd business sense.

"What's all this?" Horace asked, his eyes flinty as they settled on the men.

Gabe explained the situation. Horace frowned, mouth set in a thin line.

"Splendor's resources are limited. We can't commit to hiring newcomers over locals who need work."

Morgan bristled at his callous tone but kept his own voice even. Horace had lived in Splendor for a long time and cared deeply about the people. "With respect, sir. I believe if we put our heads together, we can find a solution."

"Morgan's right. There may be a way we can help," Gabe said. "Perhaps a public meeting to discuss how we can accommodate newcomers. More and more settlers are coming our way. We'll have to deal with them at some point, Horace. These folks seem able-bodied and willing to work."

Horace looked uncertain but didn't argue further.

Morgan's thoughts drifted to Amelia as Gabe and Horace continued discussing the situation. He knew her kind heart would ache to help these struggling newcomers. The orphanage was bursting at the seams, and he knew Martha and Amelia had discussed adding more space to the house.

Perhaps if the town could support more families, there would be fewer orphans. These thoughts buoyed Morgan as he refocused on the intense discussion between Gabe, Horace, and the newcomers.

Amelia rushed to get ready for her ride to town. After a few sleepless nights and much soul-searching, she'd come to the conclusion it made no sense to ignore the open teaching position. With her education and experience, Amelia believed she had a good chance of being selected. She also accepted her role as a cook wasn't something she wanted forever. Teaching was her true passion.

Marcus, one of the older boys, had tacked up a horse for the ride, which had taken little time. It had been a few days since Morgan had returned to town, and she expected to get in and out of town without him noticing. This was her decision, and she wasn't yet ready to share her interest in the position.

Straightening her skirts as she walked from the livery to the schoolhouse, Amelia hoped she appeared professional despite her nerves. Without discussing her decision with Morgan, she'd applied for the open teaching position after speaking with Dorinda Heaton, the current teacher.

Dorinda supported her application, believing her kind and nurturing nature would be an asset in the classroom. Amelia admired Dorinda, and hoped the interview panel shared her friend's confidence in her abilities.

Stepping inside the modest schoolhouse, Amelia was greeted by Dorinda and three other gentlemen. Horace Clausen, Gabe Evans, and Stan Petermann. After exchanging pleasantries, the men invited her to sit.

"Now, Amelia," Horace began, "as you know, we've had a few applicants for this position. Reviewing your letter to Mrs. Heaton, we believe your teaching certificate and experience at the orphanage makes you uniquely qualified to nurture and educate our youth. Your character references are sterling, too."

Amelia smiled. "Thank you, I do love working with children."

Horace continued in his usual brisk manner. "Yes, well, Mrs. Heaton speaks highly of you. But some say an unmarried woman teaching may set a bad example."

"With respect, Mr. Clausen. The town has employed single women before in this position. Plus, I believe my education and experience should speak louder than my marital status," Amelia replied, her voice even.

Gabe nodded. "Well said. Now, when can you start?"

"Oh!" Amelia gasped, not expecting an offer so soon.

"The position is yours if you want it," Gabe said. "We know how busy the orphanage keeps you, so we'll give you a month to transition."

With a look of slight annoyance, Horace nodded. "The month will give Mrs. Santori time to hire a replacement for you."

Overjoyed, Amelia accepted. This was a dream come true, a chance to shape young lives. She couldn't wait to tell Morgan.

Morgan paced back and forth on the porch of the orphanage, anxiously awaiting Amelia's return. His mind was a jumble of emotions. After pressing Martha, she'd admitted Amelia had ridden into town to interview for the teaching position.

At first, he couldn't believe she hadn't mentioned applying for the job. Frustration turned to worry when she hadn't returned by four o'clock. She'd told Martha to expect her back by one.

He'd walked outside to mount up and search for her when he spotted Amelia riding toward him. His breath caught in his throat. Even in her plain dress, she was the most beautiful woman he'd ever known.

Seeing him, she dug her heels into the horse's flanks and waved. Reining up a few feet away, she let Morgan help her to the ground.

"I didn't expect to find you here."

"Tell me how it went."

Her features stilled for a moment before a slight grin appeared. "Martha told you."

"Yep. Now tell me what happened."

A broad smile replaced the grin. "You'll never believe it, they offered me the teaching job."

Morgan swept her up in a fierce embrace. "That's wonderful. I'm proud of you."

After twirling her around, he set her down gently, his eyes searching hers. "You're sure this is what you want? The last time we talked about it, you didn't seem interested."

Amelia sighed, knowing this moment would come. "I'm sure. I've given it a great deal of thought, and teaching is what I'm meant to do. I'll miss the children. But this is an opportunity I can't pass up. It's my chance to make a difference. I can always volunteer at the orphanage. And we could see each other more often."

Staring down at her, he couldn't miss the pure joy on her face. "Yes, we could." Bending down, he kissed her.

Morgan walked with Amelia from the livery to the schoolhouse for the town meeting. As they approached the clapboard building, he noticed a cluster of men standing outside, their voices rising in evident frustration. Among them was Dutch, his exhaustion showing in the slump of his shoulders as he tried to calm the group.

Morgan touched Amelia's arm. "Wait here a moment." He approached the men. Dutch looked relieved to see him.

"These folks are new in town, looking for work," he explained. "I told them they're welcome to join everyone inside for the town meeting."

Men's voices had everyone turning to see Gabe, his wife, Lena, and Horace Clausen approach.

"What do we have here?" Gabe asked.

"More settlers," Dutch said. "Morgan told them about the town meeting."

"As the deputy said, you're welcome inside, gentlemen." Gabe didn't wait for their response before slipping Lena's arm through his and entering the schoolhouse.

Horace, Morgan, Amelia, and Dutch walked in behind them. It didn't take the three settlers long to follow.

Morgan and Amelia were surprised to see a bigger crowd than anticipated inside. Most of the deputies, townsfolk, and many of the local ranchers, including Dax and Luke Pelletier, were present. Morgan couldn't help thinking they were in for a remarkable evening.

Chapter Eighteen

Gabe stood at the front of the room, his imposing frame commanding attention. "All right, you all know why we're here. We have an abundance of settlers and very few jobs. It's time to figure this out. The town is under no obligation to create work for anyone. And several of you have told me our first obligation is to the people who've already made Splendor their home. Now, we need to decide how much help we can offer these folks while keeping the town solvent."

Murmurs rippled through the room. Morgan took Amelia's hand, his thumb caressing her skin.

Noah stood. "I'm planning to build more houses. Most of you know I have a regular crew of men who help me out, but I'll need a few more to get the work done before snow falls. I can also use one more man at the livery. I'll provide payment or food in exchange for work. Let me also say, except for the livery, these are not long-term jobs. The work needs to be finished by early December. As Gabe said, my first obligation is to locals. Afterward, I'll be happy to talk with any newcomer who's interested."

Silas Jenks, owner of the lumber mill, stood when Noah sat down. "You all know me. My position is similar to Noah's. I need men at my lumber mill, and men to bring in the lumber from my land. The work will last until sometime before Christmas. I'll pay cash or provide food for work. Locals will be hired first, then others who apply."

Dax rose, nodding at Gabe. "These are good offers from two fine gentlemen. My concern is what will happen in December. The settlers may be snowed in with no more work until spring or later. What about jobs that last through the winter?"

"Any chance you'll need more ranch hands?" Gabe asked.

Dax glanced down at Luke. "Two, maybe three. We won't know until November or December. That's when some of our people ride south to find jobs in warmer weather." Dax sat back down.

"You asked about work lasting through the winter, Dax." Gabe looked into the crowd at his wife, Lena, who offered a short nod. "Our son, Jackson, owns Devil Dancer Mine. Over the years, more land and mining rights have been added to the mine. To expand, the mine will need about twenty more workers. It's difficult work, so think hard on this before showing your interest."

Horace stood, glancing around the room. "The new settlers will have to make their own provisions for suitable winter housing. Many of you are living out of your wagons. Winters here are often below freezing, deadly if you don't have a proper place to live. For the most part, the land around Splendor is owned by many of the people in here tonight. What that means is you can't build winter shelter just anywhere. Most landowners are real protective of what they have. I'm telling you this so you have a chance to consider what to do. Some of you might want to head south, to places with warmer winters. This isn't meant to run you off. It's meant to give you a better chance of making it through the upcoming months."

The discussion continued for another hour, and could've gone on longer if Gabe hadn't brought the meeting to a close. Morgan and Amelia stayed until the end, holding her hand in his as they walked back to the livery for their horses.

"I'm going to ride back to the orphanage with you and stay the night. In the library again, if that's all right."

Amelia looked into his face, nodding. "I'll make a bed up for you."

"I'll be back tomorrow night. There are things we still need to talk about." Morgan helped her into the saddle.

"You'll eat supper with us?"

He swung onto his horse, taking up the reins. "Absolutely."

Morgan sat on a bench outside the jail the following afternoon, hands trembling as he opened the letter from his family back in Ohio. The words blurred before him as he read their urgent plea for him to return home and help with the struggling farm.

Overwhelmed, he rose and began to pace the boardwalk, his boots shuffling on the wood slats. His mind raced with thoughts of his siblings. His older brother doing the backbreaking labor in the fields each day while his younger brother struggled to keep the farm equipment working and tend to sick animals. He knew his younger sisters tried hard to keep the house clean, do laundry, mend clothing, and cook meals.

Morgan's heart ached, knowing how hard they all worked to survive, to keep the farm going after both parents had passed. Part of him longed to return, to be there for them and ease their burden.

Yet his new life in Splendor called to him, too. He loved his job as a deputy in the growing town. And there was Amelia. Beautiful and kind, she'd just accepted a teaching position. From the moment he'd arrived, he'd felt drawn to her, and over the past months, they'd grown close, a romance blooming between them.

Could he really leave her behind? Would his family be better off if he returned, or would he just become one more mouth to feed, one more body barely scratching out a living from the stubborn Ohio soil?

Morgan ceased his pacing, lowering himself onto the bench. His shoulders slumped beneath the weight of responsibility, heart torn between the family who needed him and the life he'd chosen here. He longed for an easy answer, but feared no simple solution awaited him.

Unable to contain his roiling emotions any longer, Morgan headed straight for the livery. He saddled his horse with trembling hands, desperate now to see Amelia, to unburden himself and seek her counsel.

As he rode through town toward the orphanage, doubts swirled through his mind. Could he ask her to leave behind the very children she cared for? To abandon her purpose here? And how could he bear to leave her himself?

Dismounting in front of the orphanage, Morgan took a deep, steadying breath before pushing open the front door. He could hear the murmur of children's voices emanating from the common room. Ignoring them for now, he continued toward the rear of the house, where he knew Amelia would be working in the kitchen.

Sure enough, there she stood, apron tied about her slender waist, sleeves rolled up as she kneaded dough for the evening's bread. Flour dusted her cheeks and a few wisps of chestnut hair had escaped her bun. Morgan thought she'd never looked more beautiful.

At the sound of his footsteps, she turned, surprise crossing her features. "Morgan. You're early." Wiping her hands on her apron, she stepped closer, brow furrowing. "Is everything all right?"

He opened his mouth, then closed it, words failing him. How could he tell her of the letter, the impossible choice before him? Finally, he managed.

"I need to speak with you. It's...it's about my family back in Ohio."

Her gaze softened with understanding. She gestured toward the back door. "Let's talk outside where it's quiet."

They sat together on the back steps as Morgan relayed the contents of the letter, his family's struggles, and their plea for help.

"I want to do right by them, I do. But leaving Splendor, leaving you..." He turned toward her, taking her delicate hands in his own calloused ones. "These last months with you have been the happiest I've known. I hoped...I still hope we might have a future together."

Amelia's eyes glistened with tears. Her voice remained steady. "As do I." She searched for the right words. "Morgan, I'm not ready to leave Splendor." She squeezed his hands. "I understand your family needs you. It's not fair, but you must choose the path right for you. I will understand, whatever you decide."

Morgan dropped his head into his hands, overcome with turmoil. He'd thought speaking with Amelia would bring clarity. Instead, he felt more conflicted than ever.

After supper, he read to the children, then slipped into the bed Amelia had made up for him in the library. Finding sleep elusive, he stared at the books, wishing he held even a little of the wisdom found in the great stories.

Waking early, tired, though craving answers, he dressed and rode to town. He sought counsel from another perspective. From a man he knew would offer the truth.

Deputy Hex Boudreaux sat outside the jail, enjoying the cool, early morning breeze. Hex's keen eyes softened with concern as Morgan lowered himself onto the bench beside him.

"You look like you've got the weight of the world on your shoulders. What's troubling you?"

He hesitated, then poured out the entire story. Hex listened, his steady gaze never leaving Morgan's face as he told him about the letter, his family's struggles, his love for Amelia, and her refusal to leave Splendor.

When he finished, Hex leaned forward, clasping his hands. "I know you want to help your family. But it seems to me it's time your siblings step up and take responsibility for the farm. You've done right by them all these years, sent money when you could. What you can't do is live their lives for them. It may be time for them to consider selling the farm."

Morgan started to protest, but Hex held up a hand. "Hear me out. You've made a good life for yourself here. You're in love with Amelia. If you leave now, will it really make a difference for your family in the long run? Or will you just be sacrificing your own happiness?"

He fell silent, turning Hex's words over in his mind. He stared off into the distance, feeling the morning sun warm the streets of Splendor, bringing a sense of peace.

Morgan decided to spend the night at the house he rented with Tucker and Jonas. He lay awake for hours, thoughts churning as he wrestled with the decision before him.

As morning light speared through the window, he rose and made his way to the kitchen. Tucker sat at the table, nursing a cup of coffee. He raised an eyebrow as Morgan entered.

"You're up early. Everything okay?"

Morgan sank into a chair with a sigh. "Not really. Got a letter from my family back in Ohio. They want me to come home to help with the farm."

He quickly outlined the situation. Tucker let out a low whistle. "You're in a tough spot. I can see why you're torn. Have they considered selling the farm?"

Morgan shook his head. "It hasn't come up."

Jonas shuffled into the kitchen, hair sticking up at all angles. "What have I missed?" he mumbled.

Tucker briefed him on Morgan's dilemma as Jonas poured himself some coffee. When Tucker finished, Jonas turned to Morgan.

"Here's what I think. Your family raised you right, taught you responsibility. That's important. But you can't give up your life for them. You've got your own path here." Jonas took a sip of coffee. "If the four of them can't run the farm, then maybe they should sell it."

Morgan stared at the floor. "Hex and Tucker told me the same. Maybe all of you are right. Splendor is my home now. I've got to make my own choices, find my own happiness."

Jonas squeezed his shoulder. "You'll figure it out. We're here for you, whatever you decide."

As the days passed, Morgan found himself torn between the love he felt for Amelia and the sense of responsibility he felt toward his family in Ohio.

During the day, he buried himself in his work as a deputy, grateful for the distraction it provided. At night, alone in his room, his mind raced with conflicting thoughts.

He pictured his siblings struggling to work the farm without him, the fields overgrown, and the house falling into disrepair. Guilt gnawed at him for abandoning them to build a new life in Splendor.

Yet, when he thought of Amelia, his heart swelled

with joy and hope for a future they could share. Her smile made him feel like anything was possible. He ached to take her in his arms and never let go.

Morgan wrestled with these competing desires, unsure of which path to take. Should he prioritize his duty to his family, or follow his dreams with the woman he loved? He felt paralyzed, unable to reconcile these two facets of himself.

Amelia sensed the distance growing between her and Morgan as the days passed. She hadn't heard from him, and he hadn't ridden back to the orphanage. Cole told her he hadn't left town, sharing nothing else about him. Her heart sank, fearing what it could mean.

She dreaded the thought Morgan might leave Splendor, and her, to return home. The idea of losing him now, as their love was blossoming, left her anxious and heartbroken.

Amelia wanted to cling to hope, to trust Morgan would choose to stay with her. The uncertainty of it all weighed heavy on her spirit. She felt powerless, her fate resting in Morgan's hands.

All she could do was carry on, praying he would see their future was here, together. Each passing day, without resolution, left her more on edge, envisioning a lonely road ahead without him.

Chapter Nineteen

The tension between Morgan and Amelia was unmistakable as they sat across from each other at the kitchen table in the orphanage. Several days had passed since they'd last spoken. Their once easy conversations were stilted, both afraid to voice their true feelings for fear it would push the other away.

"I got another letter from Ohio today." Morgan didn't meet Amelia's eyes. "This one was from my youngest sister, begging me to come home."

Amelia's heart clenched. They'd been over this before, after he'd received the first letter. Nothing had changed.

"Your life is here now, your work as a deputy..." Her voice trailed off.

Morgan sighed, rubbing a hand across his brow. "I know. It's just...I feel a certain amount of responsibility for them, being the second oldest. But leaving you..." He looked up at her, his eyes filled with anguish. "It's tearing me apart."

Silence fell between them again. Amelia reached

out and took Morgan's hand, her own eyes glistening. "I can't ask you to stay if your family needs you. Please understand, I can't leave Splendor either."

Morgan tightened his hold on her hand. "There must be some solution. Some way we can still be together." Even as he said the words, the uncertainty was plain on his face.

Finishing the pie she'd set out, he escorted her outside. They stood on the porch, the moonlight highlighting Amelia's auburn hair. An owl hooted nearby as they faced each other, the weight of their predicament hanging heavy over them.

"What are we going to do?" Amelia's voice was thick with emotion. Morgan reached out and gently brushed a tear from her cheek.

"I don't know. I'm going to hurt someone no matter what I do."

Amelia released a shaky breath, leaning into Morgan's touch. His thumb gently caressed her skin as they stood there, neither wanting to be the first to let go.

Their future remained uncertain, fate seeming to pull them along diverging roads.

Unshed tears burned behind Amelia's eyes. She knew how the burden of responsibility weighed on Morgan's shoulders.

"There must be something we can do," she said, desperation in her voice. "Can't we send money to help your siblings? Or could they sell the farm and join us here?"

"The farm is too much for them alone. Even with

my help, there is still no guarantee it will support all of us. Selling it may be the best choice. I wish it were my decision, but it's not."

"Then don't go. Stay, Morgan. We can build a good life in Splendor."

The tightening in his throat made it impossible for him to respond. Instead, he brushed his fingers over her hair, memorizing the silky strands.

Silence stretched between them again, the chasm of their predicament growing. They both feared losing what they'd found in this frontier town.

When Amelia spoke, her voice was soft and steady. "Then we shall have faith we'll find a way through this."

Morgan met her gaze, seeing the determination shining in her eyes. He had to believe they'd discover a third alternative, a way the family farm would survive and he could stay in Splendor with the woman he loved.

Amelia and Martha left their horses at the livery a few days later, deciding to start their efforts to find a new cook on Frontier Street. They'd left Rose in charge of the children at the orphanage, a task she took to with relish.

"We'll start at the general store," Martha said. "They always have people coming and going. Someone is bound to be interested in the cook position."

Amelia nodded, stepping up onto the boardwalk. The bell over the door jingled when they entered. Stan Peterman stood at the wall on their right, placing cans of beans on a shelf.

"What brings you two ladies in here this morning?"

It took less than five minutes to explain the experience expected for the cook position, thank Stan for passing the word around, and continue to their next stop.

As they neared the jail, Amelia's heart pounded in her chest. She didn't know if Morgan would be inside or not. They hadn't spoken in days as he wrestled with his decision. A decision she played little part in making.

Martha opened the door. The first person she and Amelia saw was Morgan, leaning against the wall near the stove, a cup of coffee in his hand. He looked up, his intense gray eyes meeting Amelia's. Her cheeks grew warm as he touched the brim of his hat in greeting.

"Morning, Amelia. Martha." His voice was as rough as gravel. Martha nodded, moving her gaze to Gabe, who had stood when they entered.

"Good morning, ladies. What can I do for you?"

Again, Martha explained about the job, asking if Gabe and his deputies could spread the word.

"I'll be glad to let people know, as will the deputies. Right, Morgan?"

"Yes, sir."

Morgan held Amelia's gaze a moment longer, his eyes probing hers with unspoken questions. Then he walked past her and out the jail door.

Amelia let out a breath. Martha took her arm firmly. "Come along. Let's keep moving."

With effort, Amelia turned her thoughts back to the task at hand. She'd do whatever she could to help Morgan. For now, the priority was to find her replacement.

Morgan watched Amelia leave the jail with Martha before returning inside for his cup of coffee. As Gabe worked, he settled into a chair, lost in thought. He couldn't stop dwelling on the discrepancies between the letters he'd received from his siblings over the past year.

The one that stuck in his mind was from his older brother. It had arrived almost a year ago. It gave a glowing report about how well the farm was doing. It said his younger siblings were healthy, working hard, and happy.

The recent letters described a very different picture. The crops had failed, the barn needed repairs they couldn't afford, and their youngest sister had fallen ill. They urgently needed Morgan's help and money to get through the coming winter.

Morgan sighed, rubbing his stubbled jaw. He

wished his older brother had been more open about their struggles from the beginning. Morgan would've tried to send them more money, or maybe traveled back for a visit. Instead, it seemed they'd kept their difficulties hidden, not wanting to worry him.

The desperate tone of the recent letters didn't match with the previous upbeat accounts. Morgan pondered over the discrepancies, wondering what could explain the drastic change.

The jail door swung open. Cash Coulter strode in, his usual smile in place. "Mornin'." He hung up his hat and coat. "You're looking mighty thoughtful this fine day, Morgan." Cash took the chair next to him.

"If you boys are going to be here for a bit, I'm going to meet Nick at the hotel." Gabe grabbed his hat before heading out.

Morgan looked at Cash. "I could use your insight on something."

"What's on your mind?"

Morgan slid the letters across the table. "It's these blasted letters from my family back home. I can't make sense of them." He summarized the differences for Cash.

"Hmm," Cash murmured as he read. "It is mighty strange. Good crop seasons and bad ones, but nothing to explain going from everything's fine to they're barely surviving."

Morgan nodded. "Exactly. And the thing is, my brother's always been straight with me. I can't figure out why he'd make me think everything was fine if they were struggling."

Cash leaned back in his chair. "You're right, it doesn't add up. Not if they're as desperate for help as these last letters say. Makes me think something else is going on here."

Morgan's eyes widened. "Like what?"

"Well, now, it could be someone else writing in your brother's name, trying to trick money out of you. Or maybe trouble with the bank forcing them off the land. Or some other threat they didn't share." Cash fixed Morgan with a steady gaze. "The point is, don't make any rash decisions based on these letters. You need to get to the bottom of what's happening back home before you do anything."

Morgan let out a breath. "I think you're right. I need more to go on before I decide whether to stay or leave Splendor. I've sent a telegram to the family minister."

Cash leaned forward, settling a hand on Morgan's shoulder. "Think of someone else and send a letter or telegram. Ask straight out how your family's doing. Find out if they're in trouble, and why your brother might've kept it from you. Decide on someone who won't whitewash it. You'll have information from two sources who have nothing to gain."

Morgan's face eased as he considered Cash's advice. "I think that's what I'll do. With information from two people, I should be able to get to the bottom of this."

Cash smiled and stood. "Let me know what you learn." He pressed down on his hat before heading off to start his duties.

Morgan tucked the letters away, his course of action clear. When Gabe returned, he headed to the telegraph office. Inside, he took a blank telegram form and composed his message to their closest neighbor, who'd also been his father's best friend.

He read over the wording to ensure it conveyed his request for information. Satisfied, he paid the fee and handed the form to Bernie.

"I'd appreciate it if you could get me the response as soon as it arrives," he added.

Bernie nodded, tapping his fingers on the counter. "Yes, sir, Deputy."

Stepping outside, Morgan felt a mix of anticipation and unease. So much depended on the replies. He hoped the responses would bring clarity, yet he dreaded what he might learn.

Morgan decided to head back to the jail for a few minutes before starting his rounds. Walking the town and talking to the locals would help keep his mind off his family...and Amelia.

By late afternoon, Morgan felt better. Visiting with those who worked and lived in town always raised his spirits.

Inside the jail, deputies Cash and Beau Davis carried on another of their incredible stories about experiences during the war. Ten years over, the war of northern aggression, as Southerners called it, still impacted life back east.

Their banter, always interesting and sometimes humorous, couldn't hold Morgan's attention. Looking up at the clock again, he sighed. Only a few minutes had passed since he last checked it. Time seemed to crawl as he awaited a reply from either the family minister or their neighbor.

Unable to stop himself, Morgan jumped up and rushed down the boardwalk to the telegraph office. Heart pounding, he burst through the door, coming to a stop.

Bernie's head was bent down as he transcribed a message onto a slip of paper. Looking up, he smiled, handing the message to Morgan.

"Your timing is perfect, Deputy."

With slightly trembling hands, he read the minister's words.

Crops struggling this year. Your family's fine but money tight. Sisters helping neighbors. Not as bad as the letters suggest. Will write again soon. God bless.

Morgan let out a long breath. The news wasn't as dire as he feared, yet his family was clearly still facing hardship. He wished he could be there to help instead of reading secondhand updates via telegraph.

Folding the paper, he tucked it into his pocket. Morgan felt some relief getting confirmation from the minister, yet uncertainty still gnawed at him.

Stepping outside, he turned toward the jail. He hoped the neighbor's response would validate the minister's message. Until then, he resolved to stay focused on his work and keep moving forward, trusting the path ahead would reveal itself in time.

Chapter Twenty

Amelia and Martha rode back to the orphanage, chatting about their efforts to locate a cook. The late afternoon sun was hidden behind a sea of clouds. Amelia found herself cloaked in a comfortable exhaustion.

As they approached the orphanage, a commotion inside made them quicken their pace. Children's excited shouts and laughter carried out the front door and onto the porch.

Dismounting their horses, the women rushed up the steps and into the house.

"What's going on here?" Martha asked as they stepped inside.

A group of children were crowded around two men Amelia didn't recognize. The men sat cross-legged on the floor, a checkerboard between them.

"Martha, Amelia." Rose walked over to them. "These nice men came about the cook job. When Mr. Amato said he liked checkers, the children set up the board so the men could play."

Amelia and Martha exchanged a smile.

"How kind of them to entertain the children," Martha said. She walked over and introduced herself to the men, who stood and introduced themselves.

After speaking with them a few moments, Martha waved Amelia over. "This is our current cook, Miss Amelia Newhall. She has accepted a teaching position in town. Amelia, this is Mr. Carlo Lombardi and Mr. Antonio Amato."

"Pleased to meet both of you," Amelia said.

The men seemed friendly enough and were good with the children. Martha showed them around the kitchen while discussing the particulars of the job.

Antonio explained how they'd owned a restaurant in New York before moving west. Their late wives were sisters and had helped in the restaurant before having children. He asked if it would be a problem if they shared the position.

"I don't see why you couldn't share the tasks. Is there a reason?" Martha asked.

Antonio's face blushed as he looked between Amelia and Martha. "Our wives died of influenza on the trip out here, leaving us with young children."

"Ah. You watch each other's children."

Nodding, Antonio seemed relieved. "Yes."

"As long as one of you is here to make the meals, sharing the job will be fine."

The men looked at each other, Carlo giving an almost imperceptible nod.

"We will accept the position." Antonio's smile was one of genuine pleasure.

"Wonderful." They decided on a date they'd start, agreeing to spend two days with Amelia before she left.

As Carlo and Antonio prepared to leave, one of the youngest girls ran up and threw her arms around Carlo's leg.

"You'll come back, won't you, Mr. Carlo?" she pleaded. "You still gotta teach me checkers!"

Chuckling, he patted her head, glancing at Martha. "Yes, yes. I'll be back."

The children waved as the two men ambled down the road, then scurried off to their afternoon lessons with Rose.

Martha let out a relieved breath, the corners of her mouth tipping upward. "Well, I'd say those men will work out well." She gave Amelia's arm an excited squeeze. "What a blessing."

"Yes, it is."

"You don't sound too excited. I thought you'd be relieved about finding a cook, or cooks, to replace you. Are you unsure about leaving the orphanage?"

"No. I'm fine with the decision. I think Carlo and Antonio are excellent choices."

"They owned a small, family restaurant in their neighborhood," Martha said.

"Which makes them perfect." Amelia's gaze strayed down the road toward town. She wondered if Morgan had made a decision to stay or leave. Her stomach seized on the last.

"I should see to supper." Amelia walked down the hall, heart heavy as she considered a life without Morgan.

The kitchen buzzed with activity as Amelia and two of the older girls worked on preparing breakfast the following morning. One of the girls cracked eggs into a large bowl while another placed biscuits on a sheet for the oven.

The chatter and laughter of the children filtered through the house as they dressed and came downstairs.

"Can you teach us how to cook, Miss Amelia?" one of the older girls asked. "Someday, I want to be a cook, like you."

"I won't be here too much longer." Amelia saw the girl's face fall. "While I'm here, you're welcome to help me prepare meals."

The girl clapped her hands together. "I'll be here as often as I can. Thank you, Miss Amelia!"

"You're welcome." Amelia finished cooking the bacon, moving the slices from the frying pan to a platter. She thought back to the intensity in Morgan's eyes when she and Martha stopped at the jail yesterday morning. It was obvious he struggled with a difficult decision.

Amelia glanced around the kitchen. "Are we ready, girls?"

"Yes, ma'am," they responded in unison.

"I'd appreciate it if one of you rang the bell to let everyone know breakfast is ready."

As the children bounded inside and took their seats, Amelia and the older girls placed platters of biscuits, pancakes, bacon, and a bowl of scrambled eggs on the table. She watched as they filled their plates. Though she prepared almost the identical breakfast each morning, she'd never heard a complaint, and there was never anything left over.

Amelia's thoughts drifted to the teaching position as she helped the children clear their dishes after breakfast. Dorinda had asked her to come by the schoolhouse to discuss her duties. It would be a good time to find Morgan and ask if he'd heard any more from his family.

As Amelia stepped outside into the cool morning air, she spotted a figure riding up the road toward the orphanage. Her breath caught as she recognized Morgan astride his horse. His usual time for riding out was in the afternoon or evenings. What was he doing here so early?

Dismounting, he walked toward the porch, his expression unreadable.

"Good morning, Morgan. How are you?"

He nodded, his jaw tight. "Not so good." He bounded up the steps, stopping beside her.

"What's wrong?"

"I sent telegrams to our minister and a neighbor to get their thoughts on how my brothers and sisters are doing."

"Did they respond?"

He stepped closer, his eyes blazing with anger and pain. "The replies came yesterday. It was all a lie. My siblings are fine. The farm is fine."

"Oh, Morgan." Amelia's heart ached for him. "I'm so sorry."

"I sent a telegram to my oldest brother, telling him what I'd learned. He responded late yesterday, admitting they made up the story to get me to come home."

His hands clenched into fists as he strode to the edge of the porch, before whipping around to face her. "I've been played for a fool. My own family deceived me." He turned away, struggling to rein in his emotions.

Reaching out, she touched his arm. "You aren't a fool. Not in the least. You only wanted to help. Your family should be ashamed of themselves."

He searched her face and seemed to find comfort in her words. With a deep breath, his expression softened.

"Thank you, Amelia. I'm glad I came here." Wrapping his arms around her, he held her tight before pulling back.

Their eyes locked for an instant. "You know I'm always here for you, Morgan."

Brushing a soft kiss across her lips, his grin was slow to appear. "And I'm here for you."

Morgan made a few repairs and stayed for lunch

before riding back to town. Spending time with Amelia and the children always lifted his spirits.

The short, terse message from his brother still weighed on him. Though not as heavy as it had before visiting the orphanage.

He'd always trusted his older brother, never suspected he might be lying. It would take a while for him to get over what his siblings had almost done to him.

Morgan was very close to leaving Splendor, and the woman he loved, to help his family on the farm. What had they planned to do when he showed up and discovered the farm was making money? Had they even considered what he might do?

Well, Morgan knew how he would've responded. He'd have turned around and taken the first train west.

He needed time to think through what to do about his family's deception. First, he wouldn't be sending any money back east for a while. Maybe forever. It was time they took care of themselves, as he'd done since leaving Ohio.

The worst part of their deceit was how it made him feel—sour on himself, and on his ability to judge people. Morgan always believed he could figure out someone, whether he could trust them or not. He wondered if the ability he'd counted on most of his life had fled along with faith in his family.

Heading straight to the jail, he slowed at the sight of at least two dozen horses tied outside the Wild Rose, and another dozen outside the Dixie and

Finn's. The saloons were always busier in the after-
noons.

Not like this, he thought.

Deciding to check what was going on, he dismounted outside the jail and stopped. Gabe and
several deputies emerged, splitting into three groups,
each walking to one of the saloons. Jonas and Tucker
weren't anywhere in sight.

"What's going on, Gabe?"

"Nothing, yet. I aim to keep it that way."

Placing his hands on his hips, he watched the
deputies enter the saloons. The piano in Finn's
stopped for a bit before the tinny music began again.

"What do you want me to do?"

"For now, stay out here with me." Gabe leaned
against a post on the boardwalk, crossing his arms.

"Have you ever seen this before?"

"This many riders in the middle of the afternoon?
It's been a while. We used to get wagons full of men
coming down the mountain from Devil Dancer Mine
on Saturday nights. They don't come as often anymore."

Morgan stood near Gabe, his gaze moving between the three saloons. "Seems a little quiet, given
the number of horses on the street."

"Too quiet." The instant Gabe's words were out, a
man flew through the door of the Dixie, landing on
the boardwalk before rolling onto the street.

Seconds passed before another man crashed
through the doors and stumbled, ending up next to
the first man.

Cash appeared on the saloon side of the swinging doors. He watched the two men on the street before turning around and disappearing inside.

"Do you want me to put those men in cells, Gabe?"

"Not yet. Let's see if Cash and Beau toss anyone else outside."

Hearing the commotion, a few store owners wandered outside. Stan Petermann walked over to Gabe.

"Where are they from this time, Sheriff?"

"I'm not sure. A few are from the Pelletier place, the rest from ranches scattered around the area. My guess is there are even some from Big Pine. Those are the ones who'll be hoping to sleep it off in the jail."

"Same as always this time of year," Stan said.

"I believe there are more than we've seen for a while." Gabe pushed off the post he'd been leaning on. "I'm heading home for some food, Morgan."

"You're going home?"

"Isn't that what I said?"

"Well, yes...but..." Morgan's jaw dropped as Gabe took off down the street.

Stan Petermann walked the few feet to stand by him. "I doubt you've been here long enough to see this."

"See what?"

"Every few years, groups of ranch hands from ranches around Splendor show up in town. They fill up the three saloons, drink, and play cards. Some get rowdy, and a deputy has to throw them out. The rule is, if you land on the street, you can't go back inside."

Morgan's mouth twisted. "Rule?"

"That's right," Stan said. "There may be more than one rule, but I sure can't think of it right now. Anyway, about six o'clock, when every one of them is drunk, wild mustangs are herded into town, and the contest begins."

Shaking his head, Morgan's gaze landed on the men in the street. "Contest?"

Stan flashed him a broad smile. "It's a sight. Drunk cowboys trying to ride wild mustangs. Except for a few bruises and scrapes, no one's ever been hurt. Guess they're too darn drunk to hurt themselves. Well, it's time for me to close up. You have a good night, Morgan."

"'Night, Stan."

Morgan lowered himself onto the bench outside the jail, leaned back, and stretched out his legs. Right now, he couldn't think of anything better than watching drunken cowboys fly off the backs of wild horses.

Chapter Twenty-One

Morgan laughed again the next morning as he thought about the previous night while dressing. Jonas and Tucker had joined him not long after Stan left, watching the inebriated ranch hands as they tried to mount the wild horses.

By the time they walked back to their house later in the evening, they were still chuckling about what they'd seen. He couldn't remember the last time he'd laughed so hard. Considering what he'd been dealing with, the rowdy ranch hands had been a welcome diversion. Now it was time to put the activities of the previous night behind him and get back to work.

Morgan felt at home in Splendor, something he hadn't experienced since leaving the family farm. He approached the jailhouse, his boots clopping on the wood slats of the boardwalk. He could see Gabe standing out front, looking impatient.

"There you are, Morgan," Gabe called out as he drew near. "I need you, Tucker, and Jonas to start rounding up any cowboys still passed out in the streets. Haul them back to jail if they can't ride without falling out of their saddle."

"Yes, sir."

He headed across the street, where Tucker and Jonas were watching the town while talking. Morgan explained Gabe's orders.

The three set off down Frontier Street, checking alleyways and the spaces between buildings. It wasn't long before they found the first cowboy, hat tipped down over his face, snoring loudly behind Finn's saloon. Tucker gave him a swift kick in the boot.

"Rise and shine, partner," he said with a grin.

The man startled awake, blinking against the sun. Tucker and Morgan hauled him to his feet while Jonas looked on.

"You best get on your way and sleep it off some-where else," Morgan advised. "Sheriff doesn't take kindly to drunks passed out all over his town."

The cowboy grumbled but ambled off in the direction of the livery, weaving slightly. Tucker watched him go, then turned back to his friends. "One down, who knows how many more to go."

The three continued their search, checking every nook and cranny. By late morning, they'd found ten cowboys, most of whom were still inebriated. They deposited all, but the three who could ride, in the jail's empty cells, ignoring their slurred protests.

Gabe gave an appreciative nod as the last cell clanged shut. "Good work, boys. Tucker, make more coffee for when these gentlemen wake up."

"Yes, sir."

Morgan walked back outside a few minutes later, ready to continue his duties around town. As he started down the boardwalk, Bernie Griggs hurried up to him.

"Telegram for you, Deputy." He held out the message.

Morgan took it with a furrowed brow. Telegrams rarely brought good news. He opened it and read the brief message:

Morgan,

Sorry about the lie. All is well. We plan to sell the farm, as neither James nor I want to work it. Come home when you can.

William

Morgan read it twice, then crumpled the paper in his fist, stuffing it into a pocket. His jaw tightened as he thought of the farm and his brother's lie. The lie causing Morgan so much anguish over the last weeks. He'd left the farm behind without a backward glance at seventeen. Morgan had no plans to return.

Part of him, a very small part, ached to visit his siblings. The rest of him rebelled. He'd broken free and found a new life. Splendor was his home now, not some farm he'd been desperate to escape.

Morgan pulled out the crumpled telegram, reading it once more before tearing it into tiny pieces. When he got to the livery, he'd toss them into the forge. His family could sell the farm and divide the money. He aimed to put down roots here, alongside

true friends who felt like kin. The farm was his past—
Splendor his future.

Morgan strode into the boardinghouse, stomach
growling. He spotted Jonas and Tucker seated at a
table near the back.

"Afternoon, fellas." He pulled out a chair.

"You're just in time," Tucker replied through a
mouthful of cornbread. "Suzanne's stew is mighty
tasty today."

Jonas chuckled and took a sip of coffee. "Don't
mind him. Tucker here thinks everything Suzanne
makes is mighty tasty."

"Well, it is," Tucker protested.

The three men laughed, settling in as she brought
over a piping hot bowl of stew for Morgan. They ate
in contented silence for a bit before Jonas spoke up.

"That telegram you got earlier looked serious.
Everything all right back home?"

Morgan shook his head. "Just my family aiming to
sell our farm. I won't be going back. Ohio isn't home
anymore."

Tucker nodded. "I understand what you're feeling.
After my pa died in the war, I just wanted to get away
from our little farmstead outside Indianapolis. Being
there without him was too painful."

"That's when you signed up for the Union Army,

right?" Morgan asked.

"Sure enough," Tucker said. "Needed a change, and fighting the Rebs sounded more exciting than plowing fields. How was I to know the war would end within a month?"

Jonas took a long draw on his coffee. "You two already know my mama died birthing my baby sister. I was twelve. After that, my older brothers practically raised us both. As soon as I turned fifteen, I lit out to join the Union."

The three men exchanged knowing glances. They'd met while training to be Union soldiers. When the war ended, they'd traveled together to St. Louis, taking jobs as deputies. Their next stop had been Austin, Texas, where they'd been accepted as Rangers. Splendor had been their last stop.

They continued to swap stories, reminding them how much they'd been through together. Morgan grinned as he listened, feeling a sense of kinship stronger than what he'd shared with his own siblings.

"I suppose we're all chasing ghosts in a way," Morgan mused. "Searching for a purpose after leaving our families."

The others murmured in agreement.

Tucker chuckled. "Destiny works in mysterious ways. Remember when we first crossed paths, joining up to fight for the Union? We were just boys then, eager for adventure and knowing nothing of war."

Morgan smiled at the memory. "The war's end caught everyone by surprise. At the time, I think we were more disappointed than relieved at the news.

Now, well...I believe we're all glad the war ended when it did."

The mood turned reflective as the men reminisced. They recalled shared battles against outlaw gangs during their days as Texas Rangers, long nights around campfires, and the camaraderie that grew between them.

"Those were some good times," Tucker said quietly. "Riding together, watching each other's backs. I felt like I was part of something again."

Jonas nodded, his gaze distant. "We were brothers in arms. Still are. Just in another way."

Morgan stared down at his empty plate, conflicted emotions swirling through him. He cared deeply for his friends, but part of him still hungered for something more. An image of Amelia popped into his head, reminding him there were still decisions to be made.

"It's time we got back to work, boys." He pushed back his chair. The others followed suit, returning to their duties with minds weighed down by memories. The past was a ghost that still haunted all three men in different ways.

Morgan headed toward Chinatown after lunch. Rounding a corner, he spotted a familiar figure sprawled in the alley behind one of the small restaurants. Hawke DeBell, one of his fellow deputies, lay amidst a pile of trash and empty bottles. Morgan nudged Hawke with his boot.

"Rise and shine, sleeping beauty," he drawled.

Hawke grunted, lifting a hand to his head. "Darn, but that hurts."

Morgan knelt beside him. "Are you all right?"

"I think so." Hawke tried to stand, getting to his feet with Morgan's help.

"What happened?"

"I found a horse belonging to one of the cowboys. I was taking it to the livery when someone hit me from behind."

"We'd better get you to the clinic."

"I'll be all right." Hawke grimaced, looking around. "Help me back to the jail."

Morgan hesitated. "First, the clinic. The doctor needs to check out the massive bump on your head."

Hawke tried to nod. "Darn, that hurts. Guess you're right."

Morgan kept one hand firmly on Hawke's arm as they made their way to the clinic. Climbing the steps, Morgan turned the knob, kicking open the front door.

"Is that Hawke?" Doctor Clay McCord hurried forward, helping Morgan deposit the injured deputy onto a table in one of the rooms.

Hawke groaned, touching the back of his head. "Feels like my skull's about to crack open."

"What happened?" Clay asked as he examined the large knot.

Hawke explained. "Didn't see who did it, but the

horse is long gone."

Morgan leaned against the door, arms folded across his chest. "There was no one else around when I found him."

"What do you think, Doc? I need to get back to the jail." Hawke asked.

"It's as bad a knot as I've seen. You aren't going anywhere for a while." Clay glanced at Morgan. "Let Gabe know what happened, then come back here. I'm going to need some help with Hawke, and Doctor Rawlins isn't here right now."

"I'll be right back." Morgan hurried to the jail, catching Gabe in a conversation with Beau Davis. "Sorry to interrupt." He explained, telling Gabe the doctor wanted him to return to the clinic.

"You go on, Morgan. Let me know what you find out."

"I sure will."

It was late in the afternoon before the doctor decided Hawke would spend the night at the clinic. By then, Morgan and his fellow deputy had discussed several topics. The one that stuck with him focused on Hawke's dedication to his wife, Beauty, and their young son, Grady.

"I fought it every way I could. In the end, I asked her to marry me. Glad I did. She's the best thing to happen to me in a long time. She and Grady. Can't imagine life without them. As soon as she learns about the injury, she'll pack up Grady and spend the night in this room."

Sure enough, when Morgan walked the short distance to the DeBell home to explain, Beauty rushed to toss a few items into a canvas bag, picked up Grady, and accompanied him back to the clinic. Partway there, he'd taken the toddler from her arms, holding him until they were inside Hawke's room.

The image of Beauty leaning down to kiss Hawke stayed with him the rest of the night and the following day. The way their gazes locked in understanding, how Grady's tiny hands touched his father's head, and Beauty's firm promise she'd only go home when Hawke could walk beside her, made an impression on Morgan.

As he headed for the jail the following morning, it came as a surprise how much he wanted what the DeBell family had—a wife who was a friend and partner, and children. He'd take a few if they were as adorable as Grady.

With the family situation settled, he knew it was time to focus on Amelia. She'd be starting at the school soon. Her days would be spent learning about the children, and planning lessons.

If he were to take the next step with her, now was the time.

Chapter Twenty-Two

Morgan strode up the orphanage steps, heart slamming inside his chest as he rapped on the front door. He planned to spend time on repairs and helping with the children before visiting with Amelia.

"Good morning, Morgan." Martha stepped aside to let him walk past her. "Are you here to help us with repairs?"

"Yes, ma'am. What do you have for me today?"

"I have it all written down. Follow me." Martha entered her office to grab a piece of paper off the desk. "Here you are. Don't worry about getting it all done today. There's probably enough work there for a week."

He scanned the list and had to agree with Martha. "You're right. This will take a few days. Guess I'd better get started."

"Have you had breakfast?"

"Some coffee."

"I don't know how you can start your day with just coffee. Amelia's still in the kitchen. I'm sure she'd be happy to fix something for you."

"Thank you. I'll stop to see if she has time." Tucking the list in a pocket, he took the hall to the kitchen.

The sound of children's laughter drew Morgan's gaze to the yard, where a dozen boys and girls played tag. He enjoyed watching them play. His eyes landed on Jacob and Marcus, two of the older boys. They were due to leave the orphanage soon, and he wondered if they'd already made plans to stay in Splendor.

"Good morning, Morgan."

He whirled around to see Amelia behind him. "Good morning."

"I also find it uplifting to watch the children." She looked past him into the yard. "Are you here to work?"

Pulling out the list, he chuckled as he held it up. "Martha provided a list for me."

"Oh, my. It's quite long. Could take days."

"Could."

"Have you had breakfast?" When he shook his head, she turned toward the kitchen. "Then I'll make you something. Eggs, bacon, and pancakes..." She glanced over her shoulder at him.

"Don't go to any trouble."

"No trouble, Deputy."

Morgan busied himself checking on the first item on the list. Patches of shingles had blown off during the last storm. He took the stairs to the basement, finding extra shingles stored in a separate room. The roof would be his first project.

Returning to the kitchen, he sat down as Amelia set a full plate in front of him. "There's more if you want seconds."

"This looks delicious. Thank you."

Offering a smile, she turned toward a stack of dried dishes.

He ate every bite, sitting back on a sigh when finished. He'd hoped Amelia would have time to sit with him for a while. Unfortunately, she had a long list of chores, also. Standing, he took the dirty dishes to the sink.

"I'll take care of those," Amelia said. "You go ahead and start on the list."

"Breakfast was delicious. Thanks, again."

After replacing the damaged shingles, Morgan paused to watch the children. Seeing him, they waved and called to join their game. He smiled and set down his tools. A deputy turned handyman could still be a kid at heart.

The afternoon sped by between play and checking off items on the list. As the sun dipped low, Morgan glanced toward the kitchen door, expecting Amelia to emerge at any moment. His heartbeat quickened at the thought of seeing her radiant face and brilliant smile.

Right on cue, Amelia stepped outside, brushing

flour from her apron. Morgan continued working, his pulse racing.

"Afternoon, Amelia." He looked up from hammering a nail into the loose step.

"Hello, Deputy," she replied, eyes twinkling. "Still working on Martha's list?"

"Yes, ma'am. I was hoping..." Morgan hesitated, suddenly nervous. He took a steadying breath. "I was hoping you'd join me for a ride tomorrow afternoon. If you're free, that is."

Smiling, her cheeks flushed pink. "I'd like that very much."

Returning a grin, relief washed over him. "Great. I'll come by tomorrow afternoon then."

"Would you mind adding something to the list?"

"Not at all. What is it?"

"There's a leak in the kitchen water pump. I thought you could see about fixing it."

Standing, he wiped his hands down his pants. "I'll take a look now."

Stopping to wipe his boots on a heavy rug, he strode to the sink, spotting the leak. "This shouldn't take long."

Retrieving the toolbox, he worked for several minutes, tested the pump, then worked several minutes more. Testing it a second time, he nodded.

"That should take care of it. Let me know if it starts causing trouble again."

Morgan worked an early shift the following day before cleaning up and riding out of town. He returned to the orphanage, anticipation building with each step. As he approached the kitchen, he heard unfamiliar male voices.

Morgan was taken aback to find two men he didn't recognize chatting with Amelia. They looked up at his entrance, conversation halting.

"Morgan," Amelia said, a smile forming. "Join us. I want you to meet our new cooks."

He stepped forward, eyeing the men warily. He hadn't expected company on what he hoped would be a private outing with Amelia.

"This is Carlo, and his brother-in-law, Antonio," Amelia continued. "They just arrived from New York with their children. Gentlemen, this is Deputy Wheeler."

"Pleased to meet you," he said, shaking their hands.

"It is our pleasure, Deputy." Carlo's gaze landed on Morgan's badge.

"We are learning cooking duties at the orphanage," Antonio added.

"I assume you two must have a lot of experience." Morgan glanced between the two.

"Oh, yes, Deputy. We owned a restaurant in New York. We will make the children happy with our food."

"I'm sure you will," Morgan said, looking at Amelia.

"I'm afraid our ride will have to wait for another day." Her voice was filled with regret. "I need to show Carlo and Antonio around the kitchen and root cellar. There's much to do before fixing supper."

Morgan nodded in understanding, though disappointment gripped him. The anticipation he'd felt for their outing now curdled into frustration. Regardless, he couldn't whisk Amelia away on a pleasure ride when her duties clearly called her here.

Noticing the disappointment on his face, Amelia moved closer. "Are you able to go on a ride tomorrow?"

"Of course." He managed a smile. "I'll come back tomorrow. It was good to meet you both."

With a final glance at Amelia, Morgan put his hat back on and strode from the kitchen, longing and regret trailing in his wake.

Amelia watched him go with a pang of guilt. She'd been looking forward to their ride. With the starting date of her teaching job approaching, the orphanage's need for her replacement came first.

Turning, she addressed Carlo and Antonio. "Let's begin, shall we?"

She led them around the large kitchen, opening cupboards and pointing out the pantry, holding cooking supplies, bowls, and baking pans. Additional pots and cooking pans were on nearby shelves.

"I store plates, platters, bowls, and other dishes in here." She opened cupboards near the pantry. "The children will set the table if their lessons and chores are completed."

Leading the men outside, she showed them the larder, root cellar, and well pump. They asked a few questions, nodding when she answered.

Returning to the kitchen, she explained the cooking schedule, when trips to town for additional supplies were made, and where she kept the shopping list.

"Breakfast is at seven sharp," she said. "I fix the same meal every morning, as I've found the children enjoy it. Oatmeal or pancakes, eggs, and bacon. Lunch is more varied. Leftover stew, soup, cold meat, bread, and canned fruit. For supper, we have roast, chicken, lamb, stew, potatoes, rice, greens, biscuits, jam. Simple, hearty fare. Questions so far?"

The men shook their heads.

"Good. The children like helping in the kitchen. If time allows, they take turns kneading dough."

Amelia continued walking them through her routine, sharing whatever wisdom she held. Though her mind strayed occasionally to thoughts of Morgan, she stayed focused. These men deserved her full attention.

After an exhaustive tour, she stopped next to the dining table. "Do you have any questions?"

Again, the men shook their heads.

"Well, I have nothing else to add. I'm sure you'll change the food to fit what you know. My advice would be to add new foods a little at a time. These children aren't too adventurous."

The men nodded. "You have a very good kitchen with many supplies," Antonio said. "We will start with what you've told us and not change the routine too much."

Satisfied, Amelia untied her apron. "We'll start fresh tomorrow with breakfast."

"I will be here tomorrow," Carlo said. "Antonio will stay with the children."

"All right. As I said, breakfast is simple and always the same. Of course, you're welcome to make changes you believe the children will like. Also, I will be leaving for a few hours tomorrow afternoon when lunch is finished."

Carlo nodded. "That is fine. I feel comfortable fixing supper for tomorrow night."

"Wonderful. Well, gentlemen, thank you for coming by today. I'll see you tomorrow, Carlo."

She stood at the front door, watching them walk toward town. This time, she wondered if the men owned a horse or wagon. Walking was fine for most of the summer, but the cold weather, rain, and snow made the trek more difficult at other times of the year.

Turning back toward the kitchen, she reminded herself how the men arrived and left the orphanage wasn't her problem. She did make a mental note to tell Martha.

Amelia looked forward to working with Carlo in the kitchen tomorrow. She was even more excited about the ride with Morgan. A ride she had no intention of putting off any longer.

Chapter Twenty-Three

Morgan reined up in front of the orphanage, lifting a hand to wave at Jacob, who stood next to a horse tacked up and ready to ride. A good sign, he thought, as he bounded up the orphanage steps, eager to see Amelia again.

After yesterday's disappointment, he was eager to go forward with his plan. Approaching the wooden door, he knocked, hearing footsteps pounding toward him.

"Hi, Deputy Wheeler." Marcus closed the door behind Morgan, racing past him.

Seeing no one in Martha's office, he continued to the kitchen. Amelia was talking with Carlo. She raised a hand when she saw Morgan.

"I'm sorry, Carlo, but I simply must be going," Amelia said. Morgan paused in the hallway, not wanting to interrupt. "It's the engagement I mentioned yesterday."

"Go...go," Carlo said, motioning with his hands.

"Thank you. I'll return before supper."

Morgan smiled to himself. He knew Amelia's "engagement" was their ride through the countryside. Amelia hurried out of the kitchen, nearly colliding with Morgan in her haste.

"Sorry," she said, catching her breath. A faint blush rose on her cheeks. "I thought you'd gone outside."

"Nope. I didn't want to interrupt you and Carlo. Shall we?"

Amelia nodded, her eyes bright. She tied on a bonnet and grabbed a light coat, meeting him at the door. As they took the steps to where the horses waited, Morgan felt his heart swell. Her enthusiasm never failed to lift his spirits. He was looking forward to a perfect afternoon ride with the woman who'd stolen his heart.

"Here you are, Miss Amelia," Jacob said with the tip of his cap. "Your horse is ready."

"Thank you, Jacob. Did you place the package I gave you in the saddlebag?" Amelia asked.

"Yes, ma'am."

Morgan nodded his thanks to the boy as well, then turned to help Amelia up into the saddle. She gathered her skirts, placing her foot in his interlaced hands. With a swift movement, he boosted her up into the saddle. Morgan admired how Amelia sat atop the horse, looking as natural in the saddle as she did walking.

After checking her coat and bonnet were secure, he mounted his own chestnut gelding. With a final wave to Jacob, they set off down the trail leading away from the orphanage, ready to explore the countryside together.

Morgan and Amelia rode next to each other along a trail she didn't know existed. The afternoon sun filtered through the trees, dappling the path before them in shadows. Aspen leaves rustled from a light breeze as they rode past.

"I thought we could ride out to Solitary Glen today," Morgan said, glancing over at Amelia. "It's one of my favorite spots around here. Nice and peaceful by the creek."

"That sounds lovely."

As they continued on, Morgan pointed out the different trees and plants along the way, explaining which ones were used for medicinal purposes, including salves for burns and rashes.

Amelia listened with interest, appreciating how much Morgan had learned about the area's natural features. She found herself relaxing, savoring the tranquil setting as they rode deeper into the countryside.

After about twenty minutes, the sound of running water could be heard up ahead. They rounded a bend in the trail, and Solitary Glen opened up before them. The small valley was dotted with wildflowers and ferns, with a crystal clear creek babbling through the center of it.

"Oh, it's beautiful," Amelia exclaimed, taking in the idyllic scene. She turned to Morgan with a radiant smile. "This was a wonderful idea."

Morgan returned her smile, pleased at her reaction. "I had a feeling you'd like it here," he said, his voice warm with affection.

They dismounted near the creek. Morgan secured the horses while Amelia spread out a blanket before removing a package from her saddlebag. Settling down together in the tranquil glen, all thoughts of the orphanage, and his duties as a deputy, faded away for a blissful moment. For now, it was just the two of them alone amidst nature's beauty.

Amelia unwrapped the package and pulled out the peach cobbler, along with two forks. Morgan's eyes lit up at the sight of the dessert.

"I hope you like peach cobbler," Amelia said a bit shyly. "Peaches are just coming into season, and this recipe is my favorite."

"I love cobbler. Then again, I love everything you make." Morgan grinned as he accepted the plate and fork she offered him.

They dug in, savoring the sweet juicy peaches paired with the buttery biscuit topping. A relaxed silence fell between them as they ate, enjoying the treat and each other's company.

After finishing, Morgan laid back on the blanket, peering up at the clouds drifting overhead. Amelia settled next to him, her head coming to rest close to his. He reached out, taking her hand in his.

Neither spoke for several minutes, the sounds of the creek and rustling leaves filling the space. They tightened their grip on each other's hand, losing themselves in this private world while disregarding everything beyond the tranquil glen.

Morgan's keen eyes scanned the meadow, taking in the wildlife around them. A red fox darted through the brush, its bushy tail flashing as it disappeared into the trees. Far above, a hawk glided in lazy circles, riding the thermals as it searched for prey.

Amelia gasped softly as a lynx emerged from the tree line, stopping to watch them. Its tufted ears twitched, listening for any sounds of alarm from the humans invading its domain. After a few moments, the wild cat seemed to dismiss them as harmless and crept off in pursuit of smaller game.

Morgan pointed toward a pine tree where a mother eagle perched, sheltering two fluffy eaglets beneath her wings. Amelia smiled in delight at the tender scene.

"It's so beautiful and peaceful here," she murmured. "Thank you for sharing this place with me."

Morgan smiled, giving her hand a gentle squeeze. "I'm glad I could show you. Not many folks know about this glen. It's been my own private sanctuary since I discovered it not long after arriving in Splendor. Now, I want it to be ours."

Amelia tilted her face up to meet his gaze, seeing the sincerity in his eyes. She could sense something new unfolding between them.

Morgan took a deep breath, gathering his courage. This was the moment he'd planned.

"Amelia, from the first day we met, I felt a connection I've never known before. Being with you these past weeks has only deepened what I feel in my heart. You challenge and inspire me, make me laugh, and enjoy life. You've opened my eyes to having a shared future."

He gently brushed a loose strand of hair from her face, his fingertips lingering against her cheek.

"I'm in love with you, Amelia. I want to spend every day by your side, sharing all life has to offer. Will you make me the happiest man in Splendor by becoming my wife?"

Amelia's eyes glistened with emotion. Reaching up, she cradled Morgan's face in her hands.

"Oh, Morgan, I love you, too," she whispered. "I didn't know it was possible to feel this way until I met you. Yes, I will marry you. Nothing would make me happier than building a life together in this wonderful town."

Overjoyed, Morgan drew Amelia into a passionate kiss, pouring all of his love into this perfect moment. When they parted, both smiled through joyful tears.

They spoke of plans for another hour as they walked, hand-in-hand, around the glen. Her new job, Morgan's work as a deputy, when to have the wedding, where they'd live. There was so much to discuss as they considered a life together. Reaching their horses, they kissed again before packing the blanket for the trip back to the orphanage.

Morgan helped Amelia onto her horse, then mounted his own. Side by side, they rode through the meadow, to the trail. Morgan reached over and squeezed her hand.

"I can't wait to see everyone's reactions when we tell them the news." Amelia looked over at him with an excited smile.

Morgan chuckled. "I have a feeling there will be quite a celebration at the orphanage tonight."

They continued chatting about plans for the wedding and their future together. When the orphanage came into view, Morgan paused, taking Amelia's hand again.

"Are you ready for this?"

She nodded, eyes shining. "Yes, I believe I am."

They arrived back at the orphanage just as the sun began its descent over the mountains to the west. While dismounting, some of the younger children came running up to greet them.

"Miss Amelia, you're back." Amy hugged Amelia around the waist as the other children gathered around them.

Amelia laughed and ruffled Amy's hair. "Yes. Deputy Wheeler and I had a wonderful ride. Let's get these horses put away, shall we?"

The children volunteered to lead them to the small barn not far from the orphanage. Morgan handed the reins of both horses to Jacob.

"Thank you, Jacob. Keep my horse saddled, as I'll be riding back to Splendor tonight."

"Yes, sir." He led the horses away, the younger children trailing behind him.

Amelia slipped her hand into Morgan's as they headed inside. The aroma of beef stew greeted them as they walked toward the kitchen.

"Mmm, something smells delicious," Amelia said.

They entered the cozy kitchen to find Carlo ladling stew into bowls. Upon seeing them, he broke into a broad grin.

"There you two are. We were starting to wonder if you'd make it back in time for supper."

Morgan gave Amelia's hand a squeeze. "We wouldn't miss it. I worked up quite an appetite on that ride."

As everyone gathered around the two long tables for the meal, Amelia and Morgan exchanged a meaningful glance. Morgan cleared his throat and stood up from the table. The chatter died down as all eyes turned to him.

"I have an announcement to make." He glanced at Amelia, receiving an encouraging nod.

"As you all know, Miss Amelia and I have been spending quite a bit of time together these past few months. And during our ride today, I asked her a very important question."

Morgan paused, taking in the rapt faces around the table. Even Carlo had stepped away from the stove to listen.

"I asked Miss Amelia if she would become my

wife."

Gasps and excited murmurs rippled through the room. Amy and a few other little girls clasped their hands to their cheeks, eyes shining.

Morgan helped Amelia to her feet. "And she said yes," he added, grinning at the children.

Cheers and applause erupted. Amy rushed over and threw her arms around Amelia's waist as the other children gathered around them.

The rest of the meal passed with excited talk about the upcoming wedding. As the children finished eating and began clearing the dishes, Morgan drew Amelia aside.

"I should get back to town."

Amelia nodded, walking with him to the door. Turning to face him, she took his hands in hers.

"Thank you for a perfect day."

Morgan tilted her chin up, kissing her softly. "It's only the first of many to come."

With great reluctance, he pulled away and strode toward his horse.

Epilogue

Three weeks later...

A light breeze swept over the crowd gathered outside the orphanage. Morgan stood tall, his raven black hair glistening in the early afternoon sun. Beside him, Amelia glowed with joy, her simple white dress showing off her natural beauty. Reverend Paige smiled at the couple as he led them through their vows, his deep voice carrying to the friends who'd gathered.

Amelia's voice was strong as she promised to honor and cherish Morgan. He spoke his vows in a gentle rumble, his eyes never leaving his bride's face.

The orphans, standing close to the couple, watched with wide eyes as Morgan slipped a ring on Amelia's finger. At the pronouncement of their marriage, cheers and applause erupted from the crowd.

The reception area was soon bustling with activity, laughter drifting across the crowd as the guests drank punch or coffee. Festive flower arrangements adorned the tables, which were laden with various dishes and sweet confections. Guests milled about, plates and glasses in hand, offering their enthusiastic congratulations to the newlyweds.

"Oh, Amelia. I'm so happy for you," gushed Rose, embracing her friend.

Nearby, Jonas laughed and slapped Morgan on the back. "Never thought I'd see you settled down, but you've got yourself a fine woman there."

Martha dabbed at her eyes with a lace handkerchief before she took Amelia's hands in her own. "We're so happy for you." Cole stood at his wife's side, smiling at the couple.

Though the festivities swirled around them, Morgan and Amelia's attention remained fixed on each other. Their eyes shone with devotion and the promise of the new life they would build together.

Making their way through the crowd, the couple accepted embraces and congratulations from their friends. They paused to admire the spread of food laid out on the tables. Roasted game hens with rosemary, honey glazed carrots, savory potato gratin, golden cornbread with butter, and an array of pies overflowing with juicy fruit fillings.

"Carlo and Antonio have outdone themselves." Amelia eyed the mouthwatering dishes, her stomach rumbling. Morgan nodded in agreement, as hungry as his bride.

Nearby, Tucker regaled a group with amusing stories from his travels with Morgan and Jonas while Ruth Paige and Martha compared notes on the latest fashions from back east.

Laughter rang out as Cole told a tale of his misadventures learning to ride as a boy. Though the guests came to Splendor for different reasons, their affection for Morgan and Amelia brought them together.

As the celebration continued, Noah Brandt spotted Jacob and Marcus lingering near the edge of the festivities. He approached the two young men, shaking their hands.

"Good to see you boys," Noah said. They'd lived at the orphanage since being brought over from the crowded Big Pine orphanage.

"Mrs. Santori told me the two of you would be leaving later this fall. I suppose she told you about the dormitories and such in town. If you plan to stay in Splendor, come and see me. I can always use help around the livery, or I'd be happy to introduce you to people who may be able to offer you work."

Marcus's eyes widened in surprise. "That's real kind of you, Mr. Brandt."

"People looked out for me when I first got here. It's only right to help others," Noah said.

The conversation was interrupted by a burst of laughter from a few yards away, where Gabe regaled a group of deputies with an animated retelling of a past adventure. While the men roared, their wives rolled their eyes.

"Quite a crew Gabe has assembled," Noah remarked to Morgan with a chuckle.

"I'm lucky to be a part of them. We've been through a lot together."

"The town appreciates all you do."

Morgan nodded. "Thanks, Noah. It means a lot."

A few feet away, Amelia smiled as Dorinda Heaton embraced her in a congratulatory hug.

"I'm thrilled for you and Morgan." Dorinda's calm voice belied her happiness for her new colleague. "Teaching with you is a wonderful experience."

"I'm still nervous, but also excited," Amelia admitted. "The children are so eager to learn."

"You're already showing yourself to be an incredible teacher," Dorinda said. "I've seen how you are with the kids at the orphanage, and at school. You have a real gift."

Amelia blushed at the praise. "Thank you. I hope I can live up to everyone's expectations."

"You will," Dorinda assured her before excusing herself to walk around.

The women shared a laugh. Amelia gazed at Morgan across the yard, her heart swelling. He caught her attention from where he stood talking with the deputies. Giving her a wink, he mouthed, "I love you," before turning back to his conversation.

Amelia smiled, her gaze moving across the yard to where Dutch hovered near Dorinda. He appeared uncharacteristically shy. Rose and Martha joined her.

"Well, what do we have here?" Amelia murmured.

Rose followed her gaze. "Oh, my. It seems the stoic deputy has taken an interest in our dear friend, Dorinda."

"It certainly seems that way," Martha agreed with a knowing smile.

They watched as Dorinda said something that made Dutch laugh. It was a rare sight for anyone who knew him. The two chatted as if they were old friends, oblivious to the observers.

"Dorinda has been hoping to find someone who shares her love of literature," Amelia said. *Dutch is clearly smitten, whether he admits it or not.* She didn't share the thought with her two friends.

As the afternoon wore on, the celebration showed no signs of winding down. Laughter and energetic conversations filled the courtyard.

Morgan slipped away from the group and came up behind Amelia, wrapping his arms around her waist. "I hope you're not too overwhelmed." He bent down, kissing her cheek.

She turned in his arms to face him, her eyes shining. "It feels like a dream."

Morgan gently brushed a stray hair from her face. "No dream could be this wonderful."

They held each other close, swaying to the sounds around them, oblivious to the continuing party.

"I love you, Amelia Wheeler," Morgan murmured into her hair.

She hugged him tighter. "And I love you, my wonderful husband."

Enjoying the **Redemption Mountain** books? Here's another series you might want to read.

MacLarens of Boundary Mountain historical western romance series.

If you want to keep current on all my preorders, new releases, and other happenings, sign up for my newsletter: shirleendavies.com/contact

A Note from Shirleen

Thank you for taking the time to read **Solitary Glen**!

If you enjoyed it, please consider telling your friends or posting a short review. Word of mouth is an author's best friend and much appreciated.

I care about quality, so if you find something in error, please contact me via email at **shirleen@shirleendavies.com**

Books by Shirleen Davies

Historical Western Romances
Redemption Mountain
MacLarens of Fire Mountain Historical
MacLarens of Boundary Mountain

Contemporary Western Romance
Cowboys of Whistle Rock Ranch
MacLarens of Fire Mountain
Contemporary
Macklins of Whiskey Bend

Romantic Suspense
Eternal Brethren Military Romantic
Suspense
Peregrine Bay Romantic Suspense

Find all of my books at: shirleendavies.com

About Shirleen

Shirleen Davies writes romance—historical and contemporary western romance, and romantic suspense. She grew up in Southern California, attended Oregon State University, and has degrees from San Diego State University and the University of Maryland. During the day she provides consulting services to small and mid-sized businesses. But her real passion is writing emotionally charged stories of flawed people who find redemption through love and acceptance. She now lives with her husband in a beautiful town in northern Arizona.

I love to hear from my readers.
Send me an email: shirleen@shirleendavies.com
Visit my Website: www.shirleendavies.com
Sign up to be notified of New Releases:
www.shirleendavies.com/contact
Follow me on Amazon:
amazon.com/author/shirleendavies
Follow me on BookBub:
bookbub.com/authors/shirleen-davies

Other ways to connect with me:
Facebook Author Page:
facebook.com/shirleendaviesauthor
Pinterest: pinterest.com/shirleendavies
Instagram: instagram.com/shirleendavies_author
TikTok: shirleendavies_author
Twitter: www.twitter.com/shirleendavies

Made in the USA
Monee, IL
06 June 2024

59479639R00134